The Scales of Seduction

Rien Gray

Content Notes

General Content Notes

Descriptions of violence (including blood, gore, and injury), body horror, societal transmisogyny and lesbophobia, brief references to past sexual assault and suicidality, dysphoria, trauma around fertility and infertility, past acts of self-mutiliation, and death of a family member by suicide (off-page).

Content Notes Specific to Intimate Scenes

Frottage, venom play (intoxication), strap-on sex, oviposition (roleplay), bloodplay, choking, cloaca play, anal sex, hemi-clit, consensual body modification, sadomasochism, overstimulation, use of sex toys, virginity kink (roleplay), consensual non-consent, dacryphilia, power exchange, contested dominance, fisting, and breeding kink (no pregnancy).

Author's Note

I did not invent the concept of Medusa's home, Sarpedon, being an island between Lesbos and Cisthene. Credit to Hesiod and Aeschylus for that one.

PERSEUS' BLOOD STRETCHED AS a glistening ribbon from stone to sea, painting rage and grief throughout the gorgon's lair. Her wrathful hands held the hero's head, masked in his gore, and Medusa challenged the gods for their cruelty again and again. Was such bitter solitude not enough? Need they haunt her here, too? She was already confined to this deep stone belly of a cave, its carved entrails descending maze-like to the bowels of the earth, a hard stomp of the feet above Hades' throne. Inches from death, yet she staunchly refused to cross that dread river of her own accord. They would have to drag her into the Styx, and it would take more than a man bearing gifts he didn't deserve for that to happen.

The red-splashed mirror of his shield irked her, an ill star in the corner of jaded vision. To think Olympus had been certain she would be so easily slain, brought low by a collection of trinkets. Medusa intended to treat them as such, turning divine gifts into decoration, their stolen light illuminating this lonesome hideaway.

Lonely, still. Aching, still.

With a curse on her lips, Medusa threw what remained of Perseus' corpse toward the mouth of the cave, caring not where it landed. No one else would see the man's pale face on this long-lost island, but his very eyes offended her, and the urge to pluck them out twitched through her fingers.

Ichor wept its way toward the water, only to be caught by the tongue of an errant wave. She watched fat red drops diffuse like oil in wax, turning the foam of the tide a soothing pink, heavy with salt. Part of her yearned to chase the strands of color, to swim and dance beneath the sun again, shameless.

But with this hero's failure, the gods were sure to send another, enacting their punishment anew. She looked down, meeting that vacant, half-divine stare, and wondered if after death Perseus could finally be of use.

Medusa remained by the ocean until it was clear and calm again, then dragged his body back into the dark to make ready.

"AT EASE, PETRA." A soft palm pressed against her brow, over the linen towel draped across both eyes. "It is done."

Relief cascaded through Petra's body. Pain answered too—a dull ache across her hips, pulsing deep into her gut—but that carried its own visceral joy, proof the kheirourgós' work was complete. The cutting had happened in a haze; Agnodice eased a bolus of opium inside of her at the very beginning, and the slow stretch of oil-slick fingers served as a welcome distraction before the fog of intoxication swallowed her whole.

Someone had cast sage leaves onto the hearth nearby. Its sharp, clarifying scent was said to stir the lungs after sedation, but Petra lived and worked in enough war tents to know the herb's true purpose was nullifying more vulgar smells: blood, bile, piss. Her senses were too strong to be fooled so easily; even with her face covered, she could trace every trail of fluid from the cut grooves and rounded edges of Agnodice's table. Subtle gutters fed a drain carved low in the floor, allowing each procedure to be cleansed away with a brief sluice of water.

Petra found it charming—fitting, even—that what nature had mistakenly granted her would now feed the soil and grow something new. She thought of red roots and damp black earth, imagined burying her hands inside it to the wrist. With enough coaxing and patience, the elbow.

"Petra?" Agnodice's voice was laced with concern.

Petra cleared her throat. Perhaps the opium had not worn off quite yet.

"I'm awake," she muttered. "Can I move?"

The kheirourgós hummed, considerate. "So long as it brings you no agony."

With care, Petra sat up, using one hand to keep the folded towel over her face. Another cloth was draped across her hips, but she saw no need to maintain modesty after Agnodice's very fingers had slipped underneath her flesh. Agony never arrived, but that was no surprise; her blood quickened much faster than any mortal line. She suspected that by evening, even the matching lines of the scalpel would be gone completely.

"You got them both?" Petra asked quietly.

She had to be sure.

"Yes. It was no trouble." Agnodice's voice carried an artist's satisfaction, the joy of standing before a new masterpiece. "Yours were a bit deeper, closer to the yellow humors than most, but just as simple to sever. The remains will be burned to Cybele as an offering, as you requested."

Such consummate skill was why Petra had come to this temple in the first place. Those sworn to the goddess Cybele, the honorable gallai, offered their services to everyone, although the expense of travel to Pessinus and a proper offering could be significant for a foreigner like herself. Countless mercenary contracts along the coasts from Athens to Thrace, fighting Greeks and Persians with equal fervor—Petra paid little attention to human borders, so long as the silver dispensed her way was pure—and then one last long trek here, to have the heavy pearls cleaved from between her thighs.

Emptying one purse to rid herself of another seemed like a fair trade. Yet the temple host promised Agnodice's expertise without taking a single coin, insisting that Idalia, the high priestess, desired a favor instead. What that favor entailed, Petra had yet to discover.

"Do you want your blindfold?" Agnodice asked.

She must have looked the fool, squeezing a towel against her face like a poultice. "Yes."

Petra held out her other hand, waiting for the length of cloth to weigh down her palm before she let the towel fall. She kept her eyes squeezed shut while wrapping layer after layer of black linen around the smooth crown of her head, then tied a thick knot at the back. Only when it was woven tight enough to stop even a sliver of light from piercing through did Petra open her eyes again, settled in a shroud of darkness.

Binding herself in such a fashion was not comfortable, but it was necessary. The tradeoff for walking among mortal kind was smothering the strongest part of her nature, lest civilization flee from her and die trying. Petra knew she could capture any human between her jaws and shatter their spine like a mouse, if she chose to. But there were too many of them walking the earth to count, and she was alone.

"My blade has scarcely left your flesh," the kheirourgós said. "Know that Attis Idalia is possessed of a singular patience. You need not rush to settle the debt, when your blood still drains and cools."

Being in any debt, no matter the source, left Petra ill at ease. "She requested my presence personally. I won't malinger when Cybele speaks through her chosen."

Agnodice's sigh was one of a physician who had treated many a stubborn soldier, eager to rise again. "Of course. The attis awaits you in her chambers. Do you need someone to show you the way?"

Petra slowly rolled her neck, popping a bubble of tension out of one shoulder. "Tell me what she wears. Fabric, perfume, jewelry."

A pause followed, the skipped heartbeat of surprise. "Linen, dyed purple. Rose and almond oil. No jewelry, but there are gold beads threaded through her robe and hair."

Cybele's wealth from head to toe. "That is the only direction I need."

"Very well." The subtle heat of Agnodice's body drifted away. "Then I will leave you to dress. Should you need any assistance, simply call out. These halls have an inescapable echo."

An interesting trait for a theatre temple where cries of pain and pleasure erupted with equal frequency. Petra swallowed a laugh, then waited patiently for the other woman's footsteps to fade into the soft clamor of the domicile.

Despite the lingering brume of sage, Petra knew the scent of her own clothes well enough to find them anywhere. She made to wrap the loincloth around her hips, only to think better of it; fast as her body could sew itself together, stiff fabric could choke the blood before reaching healing flesh. She doubted Idalia would flip up her skirt to check if anything was being worn underneath, fun as that might be. The high priestess welcomed many eager suitors, although rumor claimed Idalia's true tastes were limited to fellow sisters of the altar.

Petra's tunic had toughened after years of exposure to salt and sun, but she took meticulous care of her armor after every battle, soaking up gore with a paste of sand and ash, then working wax into every exposed inch to seal it from wear. The practice softened her palms, offering a pleasant surprise to those who made assumptions about the texture of a mercenary's hands.

Her spear and shield were retained at the temple's threshold, so she carried her helmet under one arm instead. She wore it nearly everywhere, if only to prevent bystanders from lingering on the finer details of her face or the smooth plane of her skull. The utter lack of hair on her chin and cheeks was assumed to be an ephebean affectation, while the blindfold obscured an equally polished brow.

But it felt disrespectful to enter a priestess' chamber in full war dress, so Petra accepted the risk and stepped into the main hall, seeking the scent of rose and almond oil like a hound whose mouth yearned for blood.

Plenty of Cybele's faithful enjoyed flower-soaked resins, it turned out, although there was no mistaking the musk of murex shells, crushed and strained until they produced a clotted tint, so purple the shade dared toward black. Idalia's golden beads clicked together when she looked up, the sound too low to come from someone standing.

"Women in our care usually spend days abed before walking again." The high priestess' voice was warm and heavy, curling around each word like smoke. "It is little wonder your name strikes fear in the heart of so many, Petra Kruos."

"I'm blessed with swift-healing flesh," Petra said.

If Idalia's words were smoke, her laugh was fire, a slow burn down the throat leading to greater heat. "Come now, basilisk. I know why you must hide your gaze from me, but you need not hide your heritage."

Her shoulders stiffened in surprise. "You're the first to sense it in quite some time."

Most who met Petra became enthralled by the notion of a blind warrior, like something out of a lyric poem. While there were those who mocked her or sought to test her—she meted out scorn and enthusiasm with force equal to the offering—very few pressed past that initial notion, whether she was assumed to be disfigured or legendary.

It was too much to also be a woman. And yet further still to be a monster. Who would believe so many truths were contained in one body? Mortal belief was a flimsy thing, easily strained to the point of breaking.

"Your disguise is a fine ruse, but Agnodice and I knew of your origins before she ever laid hands on you. Cybele reached out to me in a dream, and to her kheirourgós in blood." Beads clicked again as Idalia pushed her hair back over one shoulder, a reflex surely joined with a smile. "So that is why I did not take your coin."

"My silver spends as well as anyone's," Petra insisted, wary.

"I mean no insult, holy serpent," the priestess demurred, "but you seem particularly suited to help me in a certain matter."

Holy. Petra's tongue flicked in amusement against the roof of her mouth, an instinct she had failed time and again to stifle. Her kind fell from worship long ago. An ancient era of beast cults was supplanted by humanity's growing reliance on the Olympians, and what remnants survived were swiftly culled by a host of demigods, eager for glory and monstrous trophies. Entire bloodlines had been severed to singular veins, holding the final drops of apocryphal ichor: Scylla. Chimera. Basilisk.

At least she felt no guilt about cutting loose her own fertility. There was no one left in the world with whom her seed could rightfully mix.

"And what matter would that be?" Petra asked.

Another shift of beads followed, pouring over each other, a whispering waterfall. Yet her hearing was keen enough to catch Idalia's pulse behind the curtain of sound, solid and steady. She wondered what it would take to make the priestess' heart quicken.

"Have you heard of Perseus?"

Escaping a hero's name was difficult, even when one desired to. "If you mean Zeus' boy, then yes. Of course."

"King Polydectes set him to take the head of Medusa." Idalia's breath caught; gold shuddered against gold. "Perseus failed."

Petra took comfort in the fact that her face, by nature, was difficult to read. "If you intend for me to slay the gorgon in his place, you've called upon the wrong mercenary."

Although Medusa was born mortal and had monstrosity thrust upon her, Petra felt they were of a similar kind. She need not have met the gorgon in person to be keenly aware of what divine torment the other woman endured, and that was reason enough to hesitate. No payment could be worth putting a fellow serpent on the altar.

"Far from it," Idalia countered. "We only wish for you to recover what was lost. The gifts of many Olympians covered his body, artifacts my goddess has an interest in. Nothing more."

What did Cybele care for such an armory? The Greeks who worshiped her did so as if they danced on a bed of blades, treating her in one breath as a body fused with Rhea, Demeter, or Aphrodite, and in the next, an outsider sealed away from all others and outside Olympian affairs. Either way, the Great Mother's power was too potent to ignore. Yet Petra knew not to expect an answer to any probing questions—once priestesses began using "we", any hope of clarity was left to omnipotent whim—and theft didn't bother her as such. It wasn't like she'd be robbing the gorgon of necessities; Medusa wouldn't starve for lack of a shield.

"A fair trade," Petra said. "Although I find it curious you would ask after Agnodice did her work. I could have refused you and left."

"Of course you could have," Idalia admitted, although the still-water calm of her voice remained unmoved. "But sometimes the die must be cast. I would never deny you your true body, Petra, or hold that promise out of reach like water from the dying. Such bargains are anathema in this place."

The mercenary bit her tongue, teeth meeting the seal where it had been stitched together into a single blunt piece. Perhaps Idalia acted out of kindness, and perhaps out of duty, but either way, Petra was split to the bone, years of rot lancing from the marrow.

"I owe you my gratitude," she said softly; her back straightened, bolstered for the task ahead. "Where did Perseus fall?"

"Somewhere on the isle of Sarpedon, where Medusa makes her home." The priestess hummed, thoughtful. "But I would encourage you to take another night of rest before seeking her out. Your body may heal quickly, but this is a change for the mind as well."

Petra frowned. "A change I yearned for. That I spent countless years chasing."

"Nonetheless. Let your blood find its new balance." Idalia rose, her heat daring closer. Petra expected the priestess' touch, only to hear the soft click of painted lacquer on clay before a slender vial was pressed into her hand. "This will help."

Petra drew her thumb along the belly of the vial, tracing lines of familiar black glaze to the cap of wax stoppering it shut. She loosened the wax, only to grimace when a harsh yet familiar musk infiltrated her nose.

"What is this?" Petra groused. "It smells like horse piss."

"That is one of the ingredients, yes." Idalia didn't bother to veil her amusement. "But this is Aeaean alchemy, from Circe and her followers. The draught will smooth skin, thin the nails, quicken the breast. It draws from the mother's lineage. I used it myself, long ago."

For an instant, it was all Petra could do not to down the vial in a single swallow. "Fascinating sorcery."

"Indeed. I admit, I cannot be sure if the effects will act identically upon a serpent's blood, but if nothing else, it should replace the humors Agnodice drained from you," Idalia said.

If this draught did half of what the priestess spoke of, Petra would steal a hundred divine artifacts, and damn the consequences. "Do I just drink it?"

"Most women take the liquid as a tincture in wine to ease the taste, but I suppose—"

One swallow it was. Petra emptied the vial and grit her teeth against a rising gorge until the compulsion faded. She shuddered, and at the end of trembling nerves was bone-deep satisfaction, control wrought over her body after so many years of hiding inside a second skin.

Idalia's laugh was light as a chime. "You're a rather direct one, aren't you?"

Petra couldn't discern whether or not that was a compliment, but decided to take it as one anyway. "Should I know anything else about the labor you ask of me?"

"No ships will sail the waters surrounding Sarpedon. However, there is a fishing village on the opposite coast where you may be able to barter for passage of some kind." Idalia put a hand on Petra's shoulder, with a soft and yielding palm, and the shift in scent was as if a hundred roses had bloomed at once in wanton invitation. The basilisk steadied herself; it was far from the first time another woman's touch had threatened to leave her undone, even sight unseen. "But for now, return to the bed we have made for you. Let Cybele keep you in her arms one night more."

"Must I return to that bed by myself?" Petra asked.

Idalia leaned closer. She must have chewed mint and chicory; strained leaves lingered in the spill of her breath. "I will send a temple girl to accompany you. The acolytes' quarters have been ablaze with interest since the moment you arrived. But be gentle with her, Petra."

With a budding priestess? Surely. This would be a few drops of oil to salve the blades of desire, not a whetstone to sharpen herself against. "I swear it."

Idalia sent her away with a gentle push, and echoes of gold followed the mercenary long after she fell from earshot.

PETRA WOKE BETWEEN TWO girls sworn to the temple—sisters, apparently, although whether the relation was by blood or oath she couldn't be sure—and disentangled herself from the maze of sheets constructed by warm bodies. Their hearts were still slow with sleep, so she drew her blindfold down and stepped to the cistern of water in the corner of the room. After stealing one last taste of the sweet residue upon her fingers, Petra washed the glaze from her hands and face, then glanced into the bronze mirror, which was held like a sun in two chiseled marble hands.

Her reflection had not changed. On the outside, nothing had changed, yet Petra felt a strange stirring, as if a knot of muscle had suddenly uncoiled and shaken loose, or a hand around her throat relaxed after seasons spent begging for air. Perhaps the endless black void of her eyes had a new sheen, but it could have been wishful thinking, too, a trick of the half-light.

Limbs stirred on the bed behind her, and Petra tugged the blindfold up before a curious gaze could meet hers in the mirror. An indirect stare wasn't dangerous, but it was revealing, and she didn't want to spend the morning soothing some startled altar attendant.

"Are you leaving already?" The elder of the pair had a pleasant lilt to her voice, soaking the end of every syllable. "Dawn has yet to come."

Petra marked the mosaic under her feet, using each tile to close the distance between herself and the bed, soles following the leylines of chariot reins and a lion's muscled back. The beasts were Cybele's ever-present companions, proof of her wildness and power even above the Olympians. The goddess herself could never be leashed. Outside Pessinus and the greater whole of Phrygia, mortals treated Cybele with the respect once given by a certain servant of Zeus, delighted to bow and kiss her feet, only to fear what might happen if they stayed in her presence too long. Yet so many returned, time and again.

When Petra's fingertips found the hem of linen sheets, she traced their pattern toward a pillar of waiting warmth, the heavy pulses of thigh, heart, throat. "My trek will be long and arduous," Petra said, then leaned in for a kiss. Drawing the faint points of her canines—what remained from a full set of once-mighty fangs—over yearning lips provoked a shiver and gasp worth savoring to the end. "Send Cybele's grace with me?"

"Great Mother, come with mighty power, blessed and divine, she who tames all," the attendant uttered, breathless, by rote. "I beseech you to offer refuge, my gold-tressed Queen."

"Good girl." Another shiver, and a less than subtle change in the air's chemistry, made Petra smile. "Now, rest a few hours more in this lovely guest bed before Idalia comes to chastise you for keeping half the temple awake with your screaming last night."

The scandalized hiss of *you brute* was exactly what Petra wanted to hear, although she stifled her laugh for fear of reprisal. After donning her cuirass and taking her helmet from its rest, she followed the cold geometry of the temple halls out to the conjoined entryway, where her sandals, spear, and shield stood waiting. Her xiphos and its scabbard slept inside the shield, so she retrieved both, then clasped the blade to a leather strap near her right hip.

Most soldiers didn't carry their apparatus alone, burdening either steeds or servants, but Petra barely noticed the weight. There were mortals who called her build 'intimidating', although she would have blended into any Amazon warband without a second glance. The basilisk accepted the comments with bitter amusement, for no stranger could know the real danger of her body stayed hidden behind the blindfold. Nonetheless, the lines of muscle etched into her armor were not decorative; they were a warning of the serpentine strength which lay underneath.

Petra made her descent under silver throes of starlight, stitched through one last swath of darkness before the sun began to rise. This particular temple to Cybele sat in the sacred shadow of Mount Agdistis, its stairs secreted in a spiral of limestone. Each step had been cut sharp enough to split bone, but after generations of supplicants, they were smooth to the touch. Even a barefoot beggar could climb to the peak for succor without suffering overmuch.

By the time she reached the city at large, merchants were directing their wares through adjoining footpaths and raising stalls in the agora. Hearths sprung to life as bakers with oil-drenched hands turned out cakes of barley meal by the dozens as payment for pre-dawn labor: herders, haulers, butchers. Someone called for the morning sacrifice, and an ewe crooned quietly as she was lured to the altar, thanks given and libations poured as the extispex received his blade. He soothed the onlookers with prayer before slitting the animal's throat.

Offal was for omens, spread out over stone and marked by solemn hands. The long, slow stream of sheep's blood added to the menagerie Petra tasted on the back of her tongue; she knew the notes of every slaughtered beast the way philosophers named grapes in their wine. Even with her eyes obscured, the ritual played out in vivid color: drained meat butchered and divided out for the poor before the gods were delivered their portion—hefty bones draped with jewels of bright yellow fat, soaking up the rising sun and mirroring its glory.

Hunger dragged its claws through Petra's stomach. She had been forbidden all but water a day before Agnodice reached for her scalpel, and the evening fare served by the temple was paltry compared to the depths of her appetite. But Cybele's request had left Petra's purse flush with silver, so she sought out the first thermopōlion selling food at this hour.

One advantage of the basilisk's confident stride was that people moved out of her way without a formal request. She tracked the scent of glistening, crackling pork to a cook-shop with a small counter and only two seats, facing a deep divot of blazing coals where terracotta krateutai gripped row after row of iron skewers.

"A customer already?" The merchant's voice was deep and clear, the sort meant to carry over a hundred heads with ease. This early, though, he spoke with care. "My first batch isn't finished yet, but you can sit and wait if you like."

Petra could have stripped raw meat down to clean white bone with a single slice of her teeth, or grabbed the scalding krateutai with her bare hands, but after so many years abroad, the smaller rites of society had acquired their own sort of charm. "Yes, I'll wait. How much?"

"If you're carrying drachma, two each." Callused fingers tapped against a set of bronze scales. "Anything else and I'll have to weigh it."

She turned out a dozen coins without hesitation; the merchant laughed in acknowledgment, then swept her silver into an open-mouthed amphora under the counter. Every cook-shop possessed a singular music: the whisper of iron cupping clay as the skewers were turned, fire jumping to taste new flesh, a butcher's blade coming down as the beat in between. This man hummed the Seikilos verse, spicing the food to come with a husband's grief. It was a popular song near the water; most who sailed away from here never returned, for one reason or another.

Petra ate, ravenous, as the sun found its zenith and began to beat down on the back of her neck. She kissed the grease from sword-mottled fingers with the same gusto as the temple girls' essence, then moved on, seeking supplies for the rest of her journey.

Without her sight, one hawker was the same as another. They asked where she had been and where she was going, they asked if she knew about someone's soldiers at someone else's border, and each time Petra smiled and lied. It was easier to lie, to never learn their names and refusing to offer her own; she had long since tired of people who choked on the incongruity. Mortal lives were short, and she preferred to be a stranger in their minds rather than a walking myth, one of the last scions of an era long extinguished.

Most recognized her as a misthia, but that didn't matter. A band of mercenaries was unsettling in any locale, but one by themselves was presumed to be needed elsewhere, taking refreshment on the way to a larger battle. She was, in fact, although Petra knew these men draped with stately comforts could never understand how one gorgon compared to an army. To them, Medusa was an uncomfortable truth shaped into a story by time and distance, symbolic grist to mock or debate over wine while walking through the stoa.

And as far as Petra could tell, news of Perseus' death had yet to spread. No one spoke of his loss in the marketplace, nor along the broad and busy road that led out to the tradeways as she made her exit. But she wasn't entirely surprised; gods were slow to admit their failures, unless the misstep could be forged into a useful weapon against one another. At least their silence lessened the chance of some dire hero hunting Medusa down in the meantime, keen to avenge another demigod's destruction.

There was no straight path to Sarpedon. From Pessinus, Petra followed the tributaries of the Sangarios River northwest before diverting to the Euxine Sea and traveling its scythe-like curve toward Propontis and Aegean waters. The fishing village Idalia had mentioned was nestled into a craggy coastal spine, where rare gaps between its deformed ribs offered shallow pockets of seaside air and enough flat land to build on. No sailor worth their salt would risk running aground against the long marble spurs jutting from the bottom of the cliffs, not when there were safer paths around Lesbos and Cisthene.

Medusa's isle emerged from where several dangerous currents met, creating a plunging tide strong enough to drag Cerberus to its depths, if so desired. Yet the village itself lay in an almost idyllic cove, and as Petra mounted the last rough span of limestone looming over the sea, she dared to pull the barrier from her eyes and look afar.

Goats studded the surrounding mountains on small, shattered plateaus, although their herder was asleep on his feet, leaning against a wooden shepherd's crook. A host of buildings lay below, white with wear from sun and storm, but all showed signs of equal care and generations of repair. The docks were flush with people mending nets, casting spears into the water for sardines or sharks, and diving deep in search for oysters. They paid no mind to Petra's distant vigil, occupied with the treasure which struggled and gasped between their hands.

A beaten, half-made path led down the cliff, formed from ditches etched into the stone by millennia of rain and patched together by pickaxes, leaving alleys so narrow the walls scraped Petra's shoulders as she descended.

At the bottom, she savored the scintillating colors of the ocean a moment longer—water dark as wine, foam bright as silver, cups pouring into each other that would never empty—before covering her eyes again and continuing on.

As she closed the distance, an incredible clash of scents met her nose: the animal salt of sweat fused with the mineral salt of the sea; the harsh tang of piscine guts stripped from fish by the thousands; long ribbons of sandgrass stretched out and drying underneath the sun. Petra was so distracted by their bounty that she nearly made a fatal mistake.

Bodies coiled with tension as she approached, their work suddenly abandoned. The roiling weave of the nets went slack and the sharp splash of spears piercing the ocean ceased, restoring the dull roar of nature's rhythm. Their resistance in unison was threatening, a wall of rejection built around the word *outsider*, but Petra had not expected a kind or gentle welcome. She hid so much of herself every waking moment that there was no point in pretending to be anything less than the mercenary she was now; taking on a greater disguise was to court death.

"Forgive me for interrupting your labors," Petra said, "but I am looking for a man who may have come here seeking a way to Sarpedon."

Silence stretched and hardened into brittle disdain. Yet they did not need to utter a single word for Petra to hear the steady tremor of every heartbeat, the thunder of recognition. So she waited, patient and still, refusing to buckle.

"You're too late." The fisherman who spoke had a voice hewn deep into the old wood of his lungs. It took a moment for Petra to source his dialect, drawn out from the depths of memory. "He's dead."

Petra thought it interesting that the man knew with such surety. Had Medusa told the village? Had they seen it happen? "I'm afraid that does not free me of my task. I must recover what he carried with him."

Quiet, again. A smothering cloak of quiet stretched over countless frozen limbs, ready to twitch and explode if the wrong sound tore through the air. Petra knew she could kill them all with a glance, if need be, but wanton slaughter had never been to her taste. Conquest was meant to be a heightened pursuit, triumphing over a rival by finding their true weakness, not the frothing rage of brute force.

So she exchanged one tactic for another.

"Medusa acts as your mistress, doesn't she?" Petra pressed, keeping her voice low and calm. "She protects you, and you fear nothing."

"The gorgon does more than protect us," another voice chimed in, carrying the defiance of youth. "She provides for us. Even if we want to leave this place."

Someone else hushed the younger of the pair, but two breaks in the silence had sabotaged the foundation of their greater resolve. The fisherman cleared his throat and said, "You won't find any passage here. Leave and trouble us no more."

"If I leave, whoever comes after me will probably be some god's mindless child ready to burn your village and scour the sea so they can reach Medusa's lair." Petra tilted her head, muscle drawn taut along her neck, one last warning before the strike to come. "I have no quarrel with her. Let me take what I need and be gone."

"Why should we trust you?" the youth snapped. "A stranger's word means nothing."

Petra sought resolve, drawing it upward with a breath from the deep well of her belly. "Someone amongst you must have a scale-stripping knife in hand. Choose whoever carries your faith to draw their blade along my arm."

That set them to muttering, a swift but understated argument. After a moment, Petra heard the long whisper of a heavy skirt, and a wizened hand with fingers like adamant lay upon her wrist with the care given glass.

"I am Maera, mother to the pearl divers here." A lifetime of mending nets and cracking shells were written into her palm, leaving a textured map of scars overlapping one another. Her grip tightened, but it was a steadying hold rather than a rebuke. "Are you truly willing to be cut by my hand?"

Outsider or not, it was a grave violation in any honorable place to harm a guest who arrived with the presumption of peace—even a guest who might endanger one most beloved.

Petra nodded, drawing an invisible line with one finger from the crook of her elbow to the inside of her wrist. "You may. And use more pressure than you expect. Trust me."

Years had passed since the last time she shed her skin. Doing so was a vulnerable act, not only for the time required, but the sheer sensitivity of her body afterward, raw and undeniably serpentine. Light and age dulled the pale shell the longer she wore it, muddying the thousands of subtle lines that divided her scales from mortal flesh. It was easier to hide. It was easier to feel less.

In certain moments, Petra felt nothing at all.

Maera placed her knife, long and narrow, across the width of the basilisk's arm. The bladed edge found purchase at an angle, and the older woman's hold became a shackle, the kind of unyielding grasp intended to keep a sea-slick fish perfectly still. She pressed in and scraped in one slow motion, hard enough to flense through bone.

Yet only a single strip, lifeless and rigid as porcelain, came away. The blade paused, and Maera gasped, "Oh!"

"Mother, what do you see?" one of the fishermen called out.

"Serpentflesh," she whispered, yet her awe carried across the docks. "Scales the color of marble, untouched by my knife."

The pearlmother's grip loosened in startled reflex, a hand fearing flame. With it, the pressure of the knife vanished too, and Petra curled her arm inward. Even a small tear in her hide, mere inches, and the salt-thick air stung like it had found fresh blood. She drew her thumb along the gap, then bit her stitched tongue to prevent a shudder.

"You aren't blind, are you?" Maera asked, but the fear filling her voice was rooted in reverence. The sort of alarm which came from touching something—someone—sacred, out of unintentional familiarity.

"No," Petra admitted, "but if my eyes fell upon you, your veins would turn to lead. Your body would never move again." A chorus of breathless apologies spilled forth, a deluge from every corner of the docks that she pushed back by raising her voice to a shout. "But I do not hunt my own kind! Show me the way to Sarpedon, let me take what I have come here for, and you will never see my face again."

"We have a boat," the old fisherman volunteered as the crowd quieted. "Lady Medusa sends us metals and stones from deep in the earth, and we deliver anything she asks for in return. Food, clothes, hides. The merchants we trade with don't know where the gems come from."

Petra frowned. "She sails here? Back and forth?"

"That would be too dangerous." Sodden wood creaked as the fisherman jumped the gap from one stretch of the docks to another. "Sarpedon is not far. We threaded a rope from shore to shore, with stones on either end to hold it taut. When the boat is full of tribute, we change the weight and the ship ferries itself across the sea, pulled by the drag."

And so Medusa lived, untouched and unseen, the world shrunk to a single island in the middle of the ocean. Yet one island was a paradise compared to living in a barren void without end. Petra did not want to linger on the comparison. "How did Perseus find her?"

When she said the hero's name, the fisherman spit to curse him. "When we would not aid him, he swam across. The currents would batter us to dust, but a demigod... he did as he pleased. As they all do."

Petra nodded. This particular demigod, at least, had his hubris rewarded thusly. "Is the boat on your end now?"

"It is," Maera answered. "We meant to send our share out yesterday, but it rained and the tide was high."

They showed her the way. Any lingering reticence disappeared as countless hands, gentle and coaxing, guided Petra across the parts of the docks in need of mending and down the invisible step into the boat. It was kind, yet the gesture reminded her of how the extispex soothed that ewe in the agora, one final mercy before the end.

Even with aid, the balance was delicate. Their vessel was so small it lacked a sail or any other steering, and when Petra kneeled, her knees touched either side without stretching or strain. A great but joyous commotion rose as the fisherfolk gathered the rest of their goods, fitting them like puzzle pieces into what space remained. She smelled the pungent crush of olives packed next to sprawling bands of grapes, punctuated by sharp notes of pepper, cassia, and silphium, some wrapped in linen to keep their leaves and seeds from falling loose, and yet others soaked into the bodies of smoked fish, potent oils, perfumes and working salves.

The youngest among them argued for the right to move the massive stones keeping the tribute boat anchored, until Maera told those assembled to work together and get on with it. She did not so much as raise her voice, yet the effect was as swift as the Nemean Lion's roar. Petra swallowed a smile before a massive splash drowned out every other sound, and the ship trembled with new freedom.

The bow dipped hard enough to kick water into her face, but when it steadied, the vessel shot forward like an arrow, gliding across the water in one restrained direction. It went so fast Petra's acute hearing barely caught a torrent of well-wishes shouted from the docks before the splitting tide outpaced mortal volume. She was severed from the earth, afloat and adrift, but in the dark she could think of nothing but the people who had so expertly cast her away.

Hidden within the bridal bed shared by mountain and sea, the fishing village knew neither war nor piracy, not even the petty grievances of one god given sacrifice over another. They had only their distant and beloved lady, who offered the world's most opulent treasures in exchange for a simple, primal tithe. Petra understood their Greek with ease, but the connecting accent was centuries out of alignment, tongues held in suspension like amber.

Here, in a narrow, shining sliver of the world, the era she thought was long gone had quietly persevered.

PETRA WAITED UNTIL SHE could hear nothing but the crushing enormity of the sea to remove her blindfold, and even then, she did not dare look back. Thankfully, Sarpedon's shore was close at hand, and the boat continued to skim over the water and along its conjoined rope like a Titan stood on the other end, massive hand pulling over mighty fist.

To see once more was a gift. She could finally connect the aromas suffusing her nose to a mosaic of eager efforts: racks of copper-skinned fish and golden amphorae packed with oil, whereupon lengths of sun-bleached cloth veiled long green strands of herbs, stygian stonefruit like countless shining eyes, and imported ginger roots the size of Petra's fist. Beside them were nodules of incense nestled into sandalwood boxes, and she could not help but wonder who Medusa burned it for, or if the gorgon simply enjoyed the scent.

The black ash sands of Sarpedon divided the horizon between glittering sun and glistening sea. As the dark band widened, a mountain's jagged crest emerged, cutting toward the sky like the curved blade of a Minoan axe. Drawn inexorably closer, Petra spied a peculiar divot in the shore, dug too deep to be an inlet by nature, but clever mimicry of its design nonetheless. The boat was pulled unerringly into the gap, taking the place of a more obvious dock or any other evidence of the island's sole occupant.

Medusa was not waiting at the water's edge, and Petra's shoulders relaxed. That was the only detail she could not have accounted for while sailing unaware, but it seemed the gorgon did not calculate her tribute by the hour, so a minor delay from the rain was of no concern. Of course, that meant she could appear in a moment, a day, a week—and thus hiding by the boat to use it like bait was out of the question.

But the arrangement of gifts could reveal Petra's presence, and that, too, was damning. Once the bottom of the boat sank into sand, pulled like an errant lover to the waiting boulder, she stepped out directly into the water and used the tide to wash away her footprints. There was no way to know if the gorgon was wandering the island, and better to conceal what signs she could now before getting any closer.

After both spear and shield were secure on shore, she moved one open-faced crate of fruit to close the gap the villagers had made around her body, leaving an even line of boxes, pots, and cloth behind. Thankfully, the grains of somber sand were packed tightly together, allowing Petra to move along delicate dunes with a light step, mirroring their natural ebb and flow.

Her destination was clear: the island only possessed a single peak, and its exterior was too angled and rough for trees to find their roots, much less offer a space for building a home upon. The mouth of the mountain was twice her height and three lengths across, forming a maw which captured light between its gritty black tongue and obsidian jaws, stalactite and stalagmite teeth hewn to the root and allowing entry. Yet another sign of a calculating touch.

As she entered, the darkness became absolute. Petra's pupils flared, paired drops of ink amid two pitch black seas, spreading out to find even the smallest sparks of light and warmth. No clever stonework could be found along the cave walls, but the opening tunnel went on for nearly a mile before it started to subtly curve inward, forming a coil. At the same time, the floor began to tilt downward, pulling at the back of Petra's calves with every step. She kept her pace slow, silent as could be, for she imagined any sound would ripple down to the heart of Medusa's lair, dancing along the walls with nowhere to escape but whatever chambers lay below.

Blood overwhelmed every other scent. Heavy and divine, a stain that could not be washed away or lose its potency with time. Thick enough for Petra to roll around her mouth like honey, a lingering madness in the throat. For it was Perseus' ichor leading her into the depths, red and sure as Ariadne's string. If Petra looked down, she could see its radiant heat as a long, quivering line, the aching pit organ behind her mouth and nose tying one primal sense to another. Her tongue flicked out, trying to capture a deeper understanding, but stitched together, it was a single weak point of comparison.

Then she saw the thread suspended across the floor.

Were her vision not so keen, it would have been invisible. A length of gossamer stretched from one side of the cave to the other, as if some industrious spider had spun its way out of the stone and burrowed through the opposing wall. Once Petra saw the first strand, her eyes seized on half a dozen more, higher and further apart, meant to trip or strangle, with a hundred other holes surrounding them, empty as eye sockets.

And the threads were not gossamer. They were sinew. Sinew with the same god-stench as the echoes of blood on the floor, embalmed by ambrosia. Even the hardest swing of her sword wouldn't sever it—no normal blade could. Medusa must have carved Perseus from the inside out with her bare hands.

Petra knew of another mercenary hired to raid the chamber of a temple belonging to the Blémues. After long days of observation, he found the perfect moment to slip inside and traverse a chain of ladders to the very bottom, where everything of value was hidden inside a beautiful stone altar. The moment the man put all his strength into pushing away its lid, a rope had snapped and spiraled loose, opening a panel which separated the room from the desert outside. Crawling and desperate, he escaped suffocating in a deluge of sand only to be captured by the priests above. A week in their care had left him whipped to the bone; now he was a scarred wretch with an unshakeable fear of enclosed spaces.

So she considered the waiting weave in full, searching for an opening before she hoisted her spear. Petra had to aim through deep shadow and wager her toss would be true, embedding the tip in distant stone rather than sending the weapon clattering to the ground. She set her feet, took a deep breath, and imagined an odd little fleck on the obsidian wall was the defiant eye of her most hated enemy.

She wondered what color Perseus' eyes had been.

The spear flew from skilled fingers, an extension of lifelong mastery and irrepressible will. It landed untouched, wrought iron piercing her target with the muted ting of chipping glass. Lightning bolt cracks spread from the wound in the wall, but no thunder answered. No harsh and unshakeable rejection. The trap remained still, waiting for Petra to make her next move. If she could get through the threads unscathed, no other danger would spring forth.

There was nowhere else to go but forward. She stepped over the first thread with ease, but the second forced her to duck low, and the third was close enough to catch her hips if she strayed an inch too far. Petra reached over it with one arm first, body straining to balance as she arched her back, slow and sure. Since childhood, she had been unduly flexible, able to unhook her shoulders from their mooring and turn her head almost all the way around, or bend through her own legs absent pain.

With age, Petra found more entertaining uses for the practice, but it was yet another trait to downplay, a line waiting to be crossed if she wasn't careful. Warmth spread up every notch of her spine and along the drum of her belly as she pushed off her palm and lunged forward in a sinuous twist, diving over one thread and slipping beneath another. Her shoulder had barely touched the earth before she tumbled

into a somersault, rolling under a shining strand and pitching herself to the
side to narrowly avoid one last length
of sinew, held at a diabolical angle that
was impossible to read from a distance.

Petra landed on both feet, folded
into a deep crouch. With an exhale
punched out of her lungs and adrenaline gilding her vision, she rose to
standing in one fluid movement, as
if coming up for air. The threads
were untouched; her body had moved
through them like a whisper of wind,
only a brief creak of leather betraying
her presence.

A smile tugged at the edge of her
mouth. After so many years of dividing mortal souls from their bodies like
wheat from chaff, challenge had with-
ered into perfunctory duty. Putting her
talents to the test was a rare joy.

With one hand flat against the ridge of obsidian to keep shards of it from breaking loose, Petra pulled her spear free with the other. She resettled callused fingers around the worn haft, ready to venture forth before it became clear the next stretch of the tunnels narrowed considerably. They were just spacious enough to fit the breadth of her body, and only if she brought her shoulders in while pressing both forearms together, squeezing out every last inch of space. Carrying the spear, much less using it, was out of the question if she couldn't draw her arm to throw or thrust.

But perhaps that was for the best. Her shield remained on her back, and she had the xiphos at her hip to wield on the off-chance Medusa caught her in the act. The spear was better suited for an ambush; if the gorgon chased her down this passage, having a long weapon paired with the element of surprise was too much of a defensive advantage to overlook.

Petra hid the spear into the longest shadow she could find, then began to squeeze through the cramped passageway. The pressure of the mountain was implacable here; despite her strength, there was too much stone on every side to find leverage and shatter it. Her first few steps were a simple if uncomfortable task, but once Petra's body became completely engulfed by the harsh carve of obsidian, she may as well have been crawling on two feet.

Jagged ridges along the wall sunk into her armor like the careful drag of claws, warning—slow down, *stay*. Even the keen depths of Petra's black eyes, darkness seeking darkness, could make nothing out at the end of the tunnel save another perilous crevice. She pushed through, limbs straining, resisting the primal voice in the back of her mind that howled she was being crushed and could not escape.

Just as the passage began to widen, Petra stopped short, jerked backward like someone had grabbed her by the neck and pulled. The noise was worse—a sudden screech of iron on glass—before she realized the pommel of her sword had snagged against a narrow lip protruding from the wall. There was no room to retreat without risking her shield would catch as well, and trying to force the pommel through would cause another ear-splitting sound. If Medusa heard her now, she would be helpless, snapping ruined fangs into empty air like vermin in a trap.

So Petra closed her eyes and pushed the breath out of her lungs, shrinking herself as small as possible; limbless, one solid shape. Then she turned to the left, bones praying for mercy and lungs begging for air. Her shoulder slipped out into open space, pressure bleeding away when the rest of her body followed suit. One ragged inhale chased another as Petra relearned the boundaries of herself from head to toe, joints falling slack, freedom hot on her tongue again.

"Fuck the gods for putting me in this mess," Petra hissed.

Then she cursed herself again—silently, this time—for being foolish enough to make even more of a racket. The fact that Medusa hadn't lunged out of the dark and wrapped a hand around her throat could have been a testament to the cave's strange acoustics, or perhaps the gorgon had been elsewhere this entire time, in another series of tunnels or away from the island itself. Who was to say this was her only hideaway?

Petra refused to bargain her life on that faint chance, no matter how tempting. She had been mocked by the Fates too many times already; why give them more string to strangle her with now?

Especially since she seemed to be staring at a dead end.

While the narrow crush of the tunnel opened up into a much larger chamber, several times her width and twice as tall, the wall in front of her had no exits to speak of. Yet a series of deep, identical cracks ran from ceiling to floor, even and refined as etching along an urn.

The floor also possessed strange detailing, with two sets of overlapping diamonds limned around a pair of equally smooth pieces of obsidian, like a haunted star caught by dark, ominous twins.

"Huh," Petra murmured.

Groping around the wall felt indiscreet, but she traced each groove with the edge of her nail nonetheless, seeing if anything around it would give. Not one was wide enough to fit her finger into, much less find a grip on, and the rest of the surface resembled natural stone. A hard shove returned no results, and Petra knew if she put her back into it, the obsidian-draped basalt would crumble rather than yield.

Her attention fell to the floor instead. If the lines at her feet were symbols of any sort, the mercenary could not decipher their meaning, and thus the only common language between them was spoken with the body. She drew her sandal along the boundary of the first diamond, and when no devastating consequence came down upon her head, leaned her weight against the broader piece.

It sank. The diamond was not a carving but a tile, decorative and discrete. Stone and glass whispered together, an unsettling chorus in an otherwise empty room, but a portion of the wall began to slide upward, slow and careful as if someone was lifting it by hand. Petra paired each groove to the boundary of a door, which meant there were two paths forward, if the opposing tile reacted the same way.

She stretched to place her right foot upon it, and the matching section of wall also started to rise. In her travels, Petra had seen many wondrous things—a polybolos that could launch a hundred bolts using only a single pair of hands, spinning devices in Antikythera used to track the sun and stars—but those were marvels expected from the sprawling cities of Rhodes and Athens, Alexandria and Corinth. Not here, in the heart of a mountain, built by the hands of a single woman.

Humility was a less than familiar feeling. Of course she knew that Medusa was mortal once, hunted by Poseidon before seeking refuge in Athena's temple, only to suffer the spurned goddess' curse. A dose of divine sadism, now used like pomace that drunk lyricists strained into metaphor about the dangers of beauty. Yet Petra had fallen prey to the same narrow assumption—that this theft would be easy, needing little more than stealth and a clever distraction when the moment to seize the artifacts came.

Not so. Medusa's creations would have made Heron weep.

The split set of tunnels also offered its own conundrum. Petra couldn't discern whether the left or right was the faster path; regardless, either entryway would close as soon as her foot stepped off the tile. She considered diving through the gap, but if she was a hair too slow, severed limbs would be the least of her problems. Crawling in a trail of her own gore until bone and flesh knit together again was equally as likely as being pinned in place by the door and dying of thirst.

A weight was needed, something that would stay in place. Except there were no loose stones in the cavern, and even if she could somehow silently smash a wall to pry something out, it wasn't clear where the full mechanism of the doors lay. Destroying whatever pulley controlled more than a ton of solid rock would make the entire venture pointless.

With a soft sigh of frustration, Petra slipped her shield off her back. Nothing was particularly special about the design, its bronze face dented and stained from a thousand battles, bearing years of discoloration long past the point of polishing. She had replaced the leather straps along the inside half a dozen times, and worked in new studs when the old ones snapped at the neck, but it was a shield that could have stood in a line of a hundred without catching anyone's eye.

It was also the closest thing she could attach to the word *friend.*

A friend heavy enough to depress the tile so she could examine the tunnels and find what lay beyond. So Petra set the shield on the right notch of obsidian first, then let the left door close with a graceful click as her sandal slipped from the opposing switch.

Shadows congealed into pure darkness, and although she could pierce it with a look, a troubling emptiness lay past the threshold. No light, no sound, no scent, not even the faint tang of dust on the air. An eldritch stillness pervaded the space, which did not stretch forward but down, so far down that conceiving of the true depth turned Petra's stomach.

She hoped it was a trap for the unwary, some convenient pit put to use, rather than the proper way ahead. After fighting to tear her eyes from the lingering void, Petra shifted the shield to the other tile and peered down the left passage.

Myrtle leaves, pungent and vital, mixed with black storax resin to infuse the air. A human might have missed the trail, but the scent stung Petra's nose and throat, permeating the inside of her mouth. Its sharpness was familiar, resting on her tongue like a well-honed knife.

Incense. The exact same incense packed onto the villagers' ship, ground into paste and shaped with tragacanth sap. She knew without question that Medusa had come and gone through this tunnel countless times, until the smoke clinging to her skin found purchase in stone.

Petra glanced back at her shield, shook off her regret, and pressed ahead. There was no reason she couldn't come back this way and recover the damned thing, but for now she had nothing on hand to defend herself save the xiphos. Unless the next forsaken puzzle took a sword as a key or something equally mad.

The notion brought some much-needed amusement, luring a grin to Petra's lips as she moved through the tunnel, which continued to slope downward. With every step, the scent grew stronger, as did a peculiar heat pervading the atmosphere. At first, Petra took the warmth spreading through her limbs as exertion, but after pressing a hand against the nearby wall, she recoiled with a hiss. The top layer of her palm had scorched away in an instant, white molt giving way to the faintest tinge of pink. Nothing about the color of the stone around her had changed, but it was like touching the center of a blacksmith's hearth.

By the time she made it past two more coils of tunnels, Petra was convinced Hephastus himself had poured slag into her lungs. Invisible fire radiated through her sandals, pulsing in a way that made her wary the leather might burst into flame. Bit by bit, the thick curtain of darkness had fallen away, but where could a source of such powerful light be hidden this far below the earth? Petra imagined a hundred possibilities: a furnace the size of a temple, a hole bored upward through miles of basalt until it breached sky and sun, some artifact from Apollo that Perseus had kept under his belt without telling anyone.

But then she turned another corner and found the blazing truth.

She stood before the mighty chamber of a volcanic heart. Its floor was divided by a massive pool of lava, its halcyon glow burning into Petra's eyes and leaving behind twisting halos of gold. Foamy crests of pale pumice jutted from the walls and gave the room an oddly oceanic quality, but the stones were so hot they exuded their own earthy scent, like the cliffside baths where dozens soaked under the sun to purify themselves. The sour tang of sulfur lingered underneath, eating through the air.

And the *sound*. Like a thousand dry reeds shaking before the scythe, building to a crescendo of crushed glass, one high note grating over another. The earth itself boiled over in protest, but with a flow so slow and deliberate, one could easily forget the danger. Petra struggled to break her gaze from the lava, watching patterns feed into one another as liquid, honey-yellow stripes descended into red-iron gullets with bright orange tongues.

She cleared her throat. Dryness lingered when she swallowed, and no solace could be had in a room where even a river would vanish into steam. Some blackened crust of a shore awaited in the distance, but the brazen gulf was merciless, without a single island or platform to stand upon in the crossing. Save for the spumes of pumice, the walls were smooth and bleak as obsidian mirrors, offering nothing but a twist of her reflection.

And Petra feared the air itself was hot enough to do true harm. After ripping a long strip of linen from the cloth beneath her armor, she dangled it like bait inches above the roiling surface. In a blink, the fabric ignited, consumed and crumbling like an old, dry candle wick. She let the burning remnants fall before her fingers began to blister, suspicions confirmed. If she was to cross this chamber unscathed, she would have to do it without her armor.

In battle, Petra had seen soldiers die truly horrific deaths to Greek fire, not from the initial flare, but from melting flesh splitting open to sizzling fat, boiled alive in their breastplates like bulls of Phalaris. Escaping the agony was impossible when the metal was too hot for anyone to touch, fusing until suffering bones were coated in bronze. She would rather be naked as an Olympic runner than face the same.

Petra dropped to one knee and pulled off her cuirass first, leather sticking to her spine and catching on the swell of her stomach. The tunic underneath held her in an equally devoted embrace, lingering around Petra's neck, clinging to the delta between mountainous thighs, deep ravines drawing muscle from a thousand marches into sharp definition. She tugged the long drape of linen overhead and unwound the loop of her loincloth, baring herself completely before unhooking the clasps on the back of each sandal. The floor was furiously hot, threatening to scald the soles of her feet just like the palm of her hand, but Petra grit her teeth and draped the strap of her xiphos' scabbard back over one shoulder. Unlike the armor, her flesh could heal.

She had scaled cliff faces by hand before, hanging from one or two fingertips before hauling her entire body upward, chasing every narrow dip and crevice, pushing deep. Without rope or a harness, any sudden fall would have shattered every bone in her body, but that was a misery Petra could survive. Submersion in lava, on the other hand, was not. Fire paled in comparison to a volcano's innards; after a certain point, sheer heat transformed into its own primeval force.

At least it would be a quick end, she mused.

The right wall had a broad, high shelf of pumice to find her grip on. She hooked a pair of fingers around one pale protrusion, brought her palm flush with the roughest part of the surface, chasing friction, and swung upward. Petra set her other hand along the ledge, flexing her stomach to bring up both legs and place her feet along a lower, rigid lip. As the momentum settled, the basilisk's shoulders slackened, testing how much weight the hole-ridden stone would bear.

Enough—for now.

But hanging above the lava was a slow drowning. Thick heat filled Petra's nose and mouth, stoppering the top of her lungs, shortening her breath. Every inch climbing across the wall had the effort of a mile, exhaustion soaking past flesh and into bone. That she could not sweat was a faint sort of mercy, keeping both hands and feet dry as she sought one abrasive hold after the next.

After a long stretch of movement, Petra dared to look and see how close she was to the end, only to find that she was barely halfway. Acid etched deep lines into the column of her back, every segment of her spine begging for relief. Yet there was nowhere to rest, and the abutments she walked along had started to lose their shape, tapering from foot-wide platforms to narrow protrusions that descended into blood-bright flame.

She tried to bring her belly up against the wall and dispel some of the tension from her legs, only to jerk and shudder when the encroaching obsidian forced her away, hot and threatening as tar.

Petra's fingers clenched around the edge of the pumice, crushing it to pale dust. The balance in her body tipped as she scrambled to find a grip again, clawing at the blanched stone, needing friction without fracture. Her left arm was leaden with pain from bearing so

much weight alone, and when she finally secured the right in place again, the
sudden respite nearly sent her tumbling
once more.

"One step at a time," the mercenary
hissed under her breath.

One step—then hold, stay. Another change in grip, traversing the wall.
Step, hold, stay. Grip and pull. Brace
and breathe, but never in opposition.
Petra recited the rules in her head like
she was a scout on her first campaign
again, trying to knock sense past the
stubborn bulwark of a serpentine skull.
Heat did not matter; pain did not matter; focus trimmed away the edges of
the world to a single, irrevocable goal.

Her foot came down on the black
shore. Skin sizzled. The mercenary almost keened in desperate laughter only
to wrestle the sound back down her

throat and cough. No longer curled up against the wall like a beetle, her limbs forgot their peril, lighter than air as Petra scrambled past the hottest part of the floor and toward the next tunnel, praying to every god and beast who walked that the earth was whole on the path ahead.

Darkness returned, and with it the cool comfort of a sunless cage. Petra could walk without wincing, but absent agony's distraction, it was difficult not to wonder how she was supposed to *leave* this place. Medusa had created a gauntlet of death which made King Minos' labyrinth look like an idle stroll, for at least those legendary walls were open to the air, offering a dream of freedom from above. Escape did not seem permitted within this mountain, only a lull between one torture and the next.

And the next arrived swiftly. When the walls around her surged inward at acute angles to meet like the brutal point of a spear, Petra could not believe her eyes. Only a shrunken fissure remained, starting a few inches above her head, but less than half the width of her body. At a glance, she could barely push her fist into the gap—where was the rest of her to go?

But no other path presented itself. Rage struck Petra first, the notion that she had come so far for nothing, that she could see a sliver of a bright chamber on the other side without any means to reach it. In anger's wake came fear, entangled in the arms of desperation, thrashing and mindless. The adrenaline in her veins tempered to dread, slowing the mercenary's heart as if it hoped to delay the inevitable.

Through. She had to force her way through.

Petra turned to her side, standing as she would boxing in the gymnasium. During sport, such a pose hid weakness, but now she wanted to make her body a formless line, narrow as could be. She shuffled one foot forward, easing it between the walls; if she flexed her sole, the rest of the limb would fit.

But as stone pressed in around one thigh, Petra froze. The xiphos jutting from her back stole vital space she needed for mobility. Yet to end this trek unarmed against an undeniably dangerous woman was too foolish a notion to endure; Petra didn't trust her raw strength to be enough, having spent so much on the descent.

After another moment's consideration, she unclasped the strap and scabbard, and used her free foot to step into it like a harness instead. With the sword angled between her flanks, Petra looped and knotted the leather straps around that stabilizing leg, hoping the tension in her limbs would supplement any give in the knot. It wasn't an easy place to draw from, certainly, but at least the blade would accompany her.

Wedging the rest of her body into the gap felt like plugging a gaping wound with silk; the more pressure she applied, the more resistance came. Petra exhaled to compress her chest and stomach, drove her shoulder blade down into its pocket by her spine, and managed to submerge herself from collarbone to hip. Her head wouldn't possibly fit facing forward, so Petra turned until she was staring at her own shoulder, tension spiraling down the opposite side of her neck.

All she could see was black walls and thousands of hungry, polished fangs.

Shock seized her. Petra's pupils flared as she tried to make sense of the endless barbs embedded in the obsidian, now flush against her skin like a rack of fishing hooks. There were teeth, yes, lines of jagged incisors stripped from sharks and layered over equally jagged shells in a sharp parody of scales, but also thin needles of bone—long, white, scrubbed of fat and sinew. Needles whittled from Perseus' body, for they were too thin to belong to the ocean, and too rigid to be carved from a mortal frame.

She couldn't withdraw. Pulling back would rip her open, filling the space she could barely maneuver in now. Yet pushing forward allowed the maw around Petra to bite down, seeking purchase in her skin. Rigid, bloodless skin, stretched and burned and dull. The last shield she carried, hiding a soft wash of color in the flesh underneath.

Petra urged the rest of her body into the waiting teeth. Ragged strips were shorn from Petra's shoulders as she shuffled forward, pale coils left behind and catching around her ribs, connected to each other by waxen threads. Another step drew uneven lines across the front of her legs, cutting patterns. The small of her back was stripped clean. A new angle pierced the soft curve of her buttocks and carved down to thigh, calf, ankle. When she had to grip one of the walls for leverage, it lacerated old skin from between her fingers, tangling into a bracelet over Petra's forearm as she squeezed another step closer to the other side.

A cruel, crushing journey, yet not more than ten feet. She could have walked there in a blink, jumped across a pit that size with a smile, but this passage required all of her, every last inch. Fangs scraped Petra's stomach and nipped at her feet; needles captured the worn hide along her jawbone and exposed the tender scales guarding her pulse. Each time the scabbard strap was snagged or ensnarled, she wondered if her last weapon would survive the passage.

Her hand escaped into empty space, freed up to the wrist. She could not gasp with relief when the incisive walls truncated her breath, but the promise ahead fueled her, and Petra threw caution to the wind before forcing the rest of her limbs through. This was not the slow and satisfying molt of rubbing too-tight skin against a sun-bright rock, but the act of being bitten and swallowed, spit out again as a smaller, shaking creature—vulnerable.

Free again, Petra fell. First down to one knee, but the joint gave, and she ended up on her stomach instead. Panting, utterly aware of her flesh, reborn and otherwise intact. The teeth hadn't so much as scratched her, but decades of history hung like tattered scrolls from that imposing stone mouth. There was no recovering the fragments, but Petra was surprised to discover that she didn't even want to.

The last husk clinging to alabaster scales fell away as she untied the weave of leather around her leg with trembling fingers. Her xiphos remained untouched in its scabbard, as if unaware of the plight it had just endured, but when Petra stood and draped the weapon over her shoulder, the solemn and familiar weight pressed into her skin with the force of a touch. One point of contact joined by the cool caress of this new chamber, overwhelming the newly exposed nerve of Petra's body—a singular throbbing sensation, too powerful to be unwound into its thousand aching threads—until she had to close her eyes and pace her breath in an attempt to reorder her senses, one at a time.

When Petra opened her eyes again, she saw the head.

It sat alone upon a narrow basalt column which had been hastily carved, and lacked the dignity of a formal plinth. The severing of the neck, however, implied great skill, for the head was perfectly balanced, staring steadily toward the gruesome passage lined with needles. What fragile skin remained around the throat must have been gently flensed from the spine to cleave past bone, then allowed to settle back into place like the folds of a skirt.

Some mixture of lime and clear resin preserved the flesh itself, absent pallor after being drained of ichor but showing no other signs of decay, only blue chalk mottling which marked the tracery of empty veins. The jaw was unusually rigid, some last-second spasm now held for eternity, narrow lips parted just far enough to show clenched, blunt teeth. Golden hair, helmet short, ended in a sweat-drenched tangle around waxen ears. With such a stately face and cunning eyes, the graven bust could only belong to Perseus, immortalized even in death. His head was a sentinel, overseeing a room of such profound and intimate beauty, Petra felt she should have found it hidden behind the curtain of a boudoir, rather than a tapered, toothy maw.

Here the walls were perfectly smooth—by craft, not nature—and inlaid with mural-like designs that symbolized jungles and oceans, leading upward to the curved dome of a ceiling. Black touchstone was overlaid with volcanic olivine, forming dark green leaves along darker branches; tenebrescent sodalite began in layers of royal blue, imitating choppy waves as its lighter, thinner edges spread in swathes of white akin to foam; both surrounded a long reclining bed, its foundation of olive wood decorated with mother of pearl. The pillows upon it appeared to be repurposed out of nets, their weave unspun before being looped a hundred times tighter.

Around the bed were familiar remnants of offerings from the village ship: incense boxes turned into small, stacked shelves for mason's and jeweler's tools, fish racks cleaned to hold necklaces and bracelets, phials closed with old and anonymous seals, melted and recast. At the frame's feet was a chest made of driftwood, its mosaic form bearing large knots like furrowed eyes. Here the scent of myrtle and storax was so potent, it should have dyed the air or hovered above the floor in clouds of smoke.

Alluring. Fascinating. Yet devoid of their mistress' living presence.

Heat—invisible to the eyes but outlined by Petra's ophidian nose, the sen-

sory organs behind her mouth—darted to her left. She spun to meet the
blur, reaching for the hilt of her sword,
only to be driven still as a stake when
a pair of hands appeared from thin air.
Fine hands, five dexterous fingers on
each, nails buffed with bergamot oil
and carmine through artistry that made
it seem as if they had been sheathed in
blood. Ten red mirrors supported by the
slender architecture of bone, an artist's
palms, and skin as black as ink.

Not skin. Scales.

Their subtle texture captured more
light than the obsidian in the room,
thousands of small and overlapping
lamina stretching to larger, faceted
pieces as they tapered along two flexed
forearms and the throat suddenly visible between them, carried by a motion
so familiar Petra could not mistake it

for anything else: removing a helm. The high-cut cap of Hades once gifted to Perseus, drawn up and away, exposing the full majesty of Medusa's face.

Her gaze *burned*. Not solely from the gorgon's eyes—a vivid, variegated green, molten and mercurial as the heart of her lair—but the flare of jade-colored scales around the sockets and covering her brow like a long splash of dye, rising and separating into a dozen thick, serpentine tendrils which stared with equal, visceral intensity. The glow of rage in each iris was heightened by the diamond angle of Medusa's cheeks, terminating at her shapely mouth—also black (her lips), also red (her tongue).

She was unspeakably beautiful. And despite the threat, Petra could not move a muscle. No one had locked eyes with her in an eternity without being struck dead. No one had *seen* her, known her as she was meant to be.

Surprise stifled Medusa's anger, but only for a blink. She jammed the helmet back onto her head and disappeared from view, only for the force of her virulent hiss to fill the entire room: "What trick have the gods summoned now? Did Athena realize her shield was a failure? Did she trade your eyes for onyx, stranger, so you could not be turned to stone?"

Admitting that she crawled through Medusa's gauntlet of traps to steal one of the very artifacts the gorgon wore seemed ill-advised. But even if the theft was a failure, Petra had every intention of escaping this mountain alive. "I have no quarrel with you. Athena can sit on her spear and bark for all I care."

"Says the woman who came out of the dark with a mercenary's sword." The heat wafting from Medusa's body drifted back and forth in a faint, iridescent haze—she was pacing. "Who are you? *What* are you? And why should I not cut you down the center and hang your corpse like a butterfly above Perseus' head?"

Petra's throat tightened; Medusa had not seen everything, then, or perhaps she did not know to look. "I am Petra Kruos, gorgon. I am the last king of serpents who walks this earth. The one and only Basilisk."

Medusa froze. Petra could not help but take pleasure in stunning the other woman, just as she had been stunned a moment before. Yet in the wake of that satisfaction came an anxious churn deep in her gut; she hadn't considered that Medusa might not share her sense of kinship, that perhaps the greatest threat to an ophidian's nest was another who approached bearing scales.

The curtain of silence between them parted an inch as Medusa whispered, "Prove it."

A burst of laughter erupted from the mercenary's lips. "And how would I do that? You seem to be immune to my gaze, just as I am shielded from yours."

"Show me your fangs, your tongue, your tail." With every part listed, the cauldron of Petra's stomach spat another gout of acid. "Because you have come to me naked, o great king, and I see no signs of your crown at all."

For hundreds of years, Petra's pride had endured like her shield: battered daily, losing its sheen, but refusing to break. She would not lie now and pretend that she was anything but a serpent entire.

"I cut my fangs away," Petra said, and there was a strange catharsis in admitting it, rather than the upwell of shame, "and my tail, too. I bound my tongue together with stitches, over and over until it held. I couldn't speak for a month, unable to bite or chew, living off offal and raw eggs."

Silence, again, but something in the curtain shifted this time; a more painful weave, the harsh tug of shared threads. Medusa removed the helm of Hades once more, and the raging fire in her eyes had died down to ashen horror.

"Why?"

The basilisk's smile was a crescent flash of teeth, brief and cutting. "Why do you live on this island? Not only isolated from the rest of the world by the sea, but beneath the earth and a massive mountain of stone. In its scorched and blistering omphalos."

"Because—" Sparks of anger appeared again, but they were reflexive, pressed out of an old, still-burning wound. "I am hunted, still. It does not matter if I am kind or cruel. It does not matter if I make sacrifice or curse the gods. That I continue to breathe is an insult. That they cannot hold my power between their hands and use it against others wounds their pride. Mortal or divine, they want my eyes, my head... but the rest of me does not matter."

"I could not bear to be alone," Petra said in answer, "but my kind is gone. There is no one to seek refuge with. So I forced myself into a human shape."

The gorgon took a step closer, Hades' helmet hanging from her fingertips like it was any other piece of armor. "How did you hide your scales? That stunning white, accented with reds and pinks. I look at you and see blood smeared across a temple floor."

Medusa's tone fused the words into a compliment; heat wrapped around the back of Petra's neck and pulled. "Old skin dulls under the sun and blurs the lines. I spent years inside that cage of flesh, refusing to shed, feeling it wither and tighten. Going numb. But then your traps stripped me clean. You're the first to see this color in a very long time."

Malachite eyes flickered up and down the length of Petra's body before that green and glorious attention deflected to Perseus' solemn head. "Before he came, the tunnels were empty. I thought the distance alone would convince any interlopers to consider my solitude, how little danger I presented. But, no... that *hero* walked miles down into the earth to try and slit my throat in my sleep. If a nightmare hadn't left me restless, who knows what might have happened."

Petra saw what could have been in a vivid splash across her mind: the fine scales along Medusa's neck split asunder; splashed red, shattered black, Perseus' fingers fitting into the gap to snap her spine and break the last connection of flesh. Her head raised high, trailing threads of gore, body falling at his feet. Not a woman, just power to be caught between the hands and unstoppered, same as any bottle.

It was a blessing the trials in the mountain had burned through Petra's last meal; the jolt of sickness in her gut cast acid up her throat and nothing more.

"I did not intend to make the same mistake twice," Medusa continued. "So I ripped the stone open and made this mountain in my image anew. I transformed his body into a message, a warning. That anyone who sought me out might know a fraction, a single arduous drop, of the pain I endure every waking moment."

She projected unfettered dominance: mistress of the labyrinth, mistress of the house. Every trap Petra had endured or subdued was crafted by Medusa's hands, cruelty by design, touch by proxy. A suffocating tapestry of pain, punctuated by the true dread of failure. Yet no spite rose in the mercenary's breast.

"I know," Petra said, then dared to add, "I understand."

"If you understand, then why are you *here*?"

A step too far. Rage coated Medusa's tongue, sure as venom, the rejection in her throat like the squeeze of a gland. Silence was good as admitting guilt, and no lie would serve.

"Not to kill you," Petra began. "Not to do anything to you. A priestess of Cybele asked—"

Carmine nails bit into the band of Hades' helm, and Medusa's *tsk* of denial was paired with a sharp turn of her head. "Another goddess. Of course."

"The temple gave me something I had dreamed of for years," the mercenary snapped. "Something I could find no other way to do to myself. And all they asked in return was for me to come here and recover what was lost."

"And what was lost, hm?" Medusa's lip curled in ire. "What have I taken from you?"

Nothing. Yet Petra glanced at the helmet in the gorgon's grasp, and that look alone was enough for Medusa to place it on Perseus' head in one aggrieved gesture. It seemed the artifact did not know life from death; his cold, soulless face vanished from sight, although the pillar holding him remained untouched.

"That's usually where I keep it," Medusa noted idly. "I hate the idea of him looking at me, trophy or not."

Thus Petra understood the chamber anew. The frame holding a waist-high mirror above a basin for ablutions was wound around the reflective bronze of Athena's shield; the hefty purse of leather and sinew at the foot of Medusa's bed, stippled with feathers, was a kibisis holding Hermes' sandals. Every godly gift turned to common purpose—the only one Petra could not spy among them was the blade.

"Yes, basilisk." There was a certain lilt in the way Medusa referred to her, tongue wrought with cunning. "I, too, have a sword. Are you asking yourself if I can reach it before you draw your own?"

Petra's lips pursed. "I said I did not come here to harm you."

"Intention and instinct are two very different things," Medusa said.

She stood empty-handed. The dark drape of her chiton was thin enough to see through, although only one shoulder had been pinned, leaving the other bare down to the supple line of her breast, stygian muscle softening to shades of laurel. The strophion above Medusa's waist was too narrow to hide a knife, made from a flat black cord shot through with vivid red thread, serving only to sharpen the flare of her hips.

Petra knew how to play the brigand. How a sudden harsh threat and brandishing her weapon could startle someone long enough to make off with their valuables. She could sling the kibisis over her shoulder, rip the shield from its mooring, and snatch the cap off Perseus' head, all before the swiftest sprinter could take a single step. Escaping would be more of a trial, but if she no longer cared for stealth, brute force would shatter obsidian like any other glass.

But was that why she was here? Had she suffered so much just to become a petty thief?

"I wanted to meet you," Petra whispered, then called more force to her voice. "I had to know if you were anything like me."

Intrigue put a new sheen on Medusa's eyes—not the bright glint of anger, but a warm shine like gold. The serpents atop her head slackened, their round green noses brushing against her shoulders. "And what is your verdict, Petra Kruos? Am I?"

A terrifying question, but worth every sacrifice for the answer. "Let's find out."

Petra lunged to the right. Not at Medusa, but between her and Perseus' head, where the helm lay hidden. The gorgon jolted toward her means of escape, only to collide into the solid counter of the mercenary's body. Solid, but sensitive. Petra nearly bit through her tongue as the two of them toppled to the floor, shocked by the warmth pressed against her from shoulder to hip, sultry and welcome as the sun. Wiry strength struggled against her own as they grappled breast to breast, before Petra hooked one leg around Medusa's and flipped the other woman onto her back to pin her in place.

Trapping the gorgon's wrists against the floor should have given Petra a moment to catch her breath. Yet before new air could enter her lungs, one of Medusa's serpents lashed out, sinking needle-thin fangs into the side of Petra's neck. The bite was brief, but hit a vital nerve with such force and accuracy that it rebounded through her blood like a lightning bolt cast straight from Zeus' hand. Her fingers went slack, vision lost to shaking, iridescent silver, and a powerful twist of Medusa's hips sent Petra sprawling across the stone.

Panting and briefly delirious, she felt around the mark at her throat. The split flesh was healing already, but a hard, heavy throb lingered under her skin, hot and pushing deeper. As she stood and her eyes cleared, Medusa was crouched low, thighs folded and weight perched against her right hand, leaving the rest of her ready to uncoil and strike.

"You have true venom," Petra rasped.

"It won't hurt you." Medusa's smile bared the full line of her fangs. "Much."

Despite taking two temple girls in one bed, Petra had not let either of them touch her in more than a cursory fashion. There were many ways to find pleasure, of course, but it was easier to play into assumptions of dominance rather than pretending at her own bliss. Their satisfaction was enough. Or, at least, better than struggling against the discomfort of her desiccated skin for hours on end. The notion of an invulnerable, implacable woman remained an easy phantom to conjure around herself: sovereign, stoic, stone.

Yet Medusa had pierced her through without a breath of hesitation. Even as the shallow gouge of the gorgon's bite sealed and Petra's blood distilled the venom, an echo remained, a permanent mark of claim. No other opponent had ever come close; no other lover would have dared. What could have been taken as either a threat or flirtation settled in Petra's body as a sudden, visceral reckoning.

If Medusa could do that much to her with a single touch, what else could she do?

Those deep-set chalcedony eyes no longer shone with shock or rage. They presented a new and even more compelling facet: *challenge*. The will to struggle together, and see which one of them could earn victory.

Petra lunged again. Lower this time, as not to give her rival the advantage of gravity. It was a calculated dive, one Petra had articulated with ease in the gauntlet of Perseus' sinews, but the gorgon was not a stationary target. Medusa darted to the side, slipping the attempted hook around her arm with another swift twist, yet the gap was closed. Petra's other hand seized one ankle, then yanked the gorgon toward her like a huntress' snare.

A wide kick brushed the cap of Petra's shoulder, distracting but ineffective. When she made a grab for that leg too, Medusa snarled and spun the opposite way, so that the basilisk's fingers captured fabric instead of flesh. Less of an anchor than she wanted, but an anchor nonetheless. She pulled to bring their bodies together, and the pin of Medusa's chiton threatened to snap, a sharp needle of bronze trapped in a weave of black.

"You must have been a terror in the palaestra." Medusa's breath quickened as she fought to get free, giving her voice a new and intoxicating inflection. "The way you move, I bet wrestlers twice your size couldn't stop you."

Yet as Petra made to hook her calf around Medusa's for a proper lock, the gorgon slipped loose with another quick pivot, making the mercenary growl, "And *you* move like someone dipped you head to toe in oil."

"If you plan to catch me, you have to earn it," Medusa snarled, an instant before another serpentine head sank its fangs into Petra's wrist.

The pain was brief, the surrounding numbness familiar, but a second dose of venom in quick succession intensified the ache throughout her entire body. Mercury swallowed the basilisk's vision again, waves pulsing in time with the quick-trample beat of Petra's heart. Yet nothing could surpass the sensation of Medusa's lithe form struggling against hers, and she did not need to see to wrap a leg over one thrashing calf, then another. Petra bent her knees outward, parting Medusa's legs like a pair of straining wings, and the gorgon's answering gasp echoed off the ceiling.

Another bite was sure to come, but when Medusa arched her back, fighting for leverage, Petra hissed between clenched teeth. The scratch of linen against the narrow peaks of her chest should have gone unnoticed as a split second of friction; instead, twin lines of heat shot straight down between flexed thighs, where a dual ache answered. Whether it was from the molt or that blossoming brew Agnodice had given her, she couldn't be sure, but in tandem with the venom, Petra's focus was fraying by the second.

If the gorgon planned to boil her blood, doing the same became the only possible rebuke.

Even with her sight recovering in fits and starts, the world before Petra was swallowed by shimmering coils and lustrous fangs. Medusa clawed toward her face as another serpent struck; Petra accepted the scratch from the former to dodge the latter, making space with an uncanny turn of her head, and thrust one arm underneath Medusa's, elbow wedged against her ribs. She reached across the gorgon's chest, completing her hold by grasping the opposite wrist, before that hand seized the writhing snakes and gathered them in the circle of her fingers like a sheaf of wheat. Their enraged hissing was a deafening chorus, but held by the throat, it was impossible to bend and bite in retribution.

"You—" Equally trapped within the diamond of Petra's arms and legs, Medusa's hips bucked to no avail. "Now neither of us can get anywhere."

That was true. With the basilisk's body knotted around the gorgon's like seaweed, they were too bound up in one another to press an advantage or escape. Yet Petra flexed another inch, just enough to make Medusa cry out, pushing for that point of surrender, submission, connection.

She had to be in control. She needed control, but something about the other woman threatened to unravel that desire from the inside out.

The supple limbs ensnared by hers suddenly went slack. Petra knew she could take advantage and pull even harder, but there was nowhere to go, and expending so much energy without purpose was sure to tilt the advantage Medusa's way. Locked together on the floor, they regained their breath together, belly to back. The heat of exertion faded, yet Medusa still painted a scorching line from Petra's shoulder to hip, the thin weave of fabric separating scale from scale more of a tease than true division.

"Tell me, basilisk," Medusa whispered, "if you are the king of serpents, does that make me your queen?"

Petra could have laughed, howled, or lost her mind at the notion. Would that the venom still burned in her veins and could have taken the blame, but this eagerness was hers alone. "You can be. But we have no lands to call our own, and the crowns were melted down long ago."

"What a shame." The serpents atop Medusa's head echoed her grief, tongues flickering out, draping over Petra's fingers like a fainting couch.

"Then I must find such majesty else-where."

Medusa shifted, too fluid to follow or catch, and Petra only understood the gorgon's true dexterity an instant before full lips captured hers, tongue plunging deep. A stilted sound erupted from the basilisk's throat, the moan of an animal stunned for sacrifice with a single, sharp blow. She almost choked on the force of her own need, de-sire drowning out every other thought, staining every long-abandoned space inside her soul.

Air was irrelevant. Petra returned the kiss as if frenzied, biting, tasting; Medusa's mouth swelled, mirroring the ache. A thousand-year hunger found an unmatched feast, thirst slaked to the point of intoxication, dizzying and damning.

Then the forked tip of Medusa's tongue sought her own and met one solid piece. Petra's shoulders went rigid, recoil crushing strands of muscle along the back of her neck as she fought not to fumble. She couldn't honor the contact the way she wanted with such a blunt and dull instrument, no longer a bident piercing through, capturing taste and knowledge in equal measure. One vital sense, completely shuttered.

And the gorgon had felt it too, Petra knew. How would Medusa not? She could trace the line of the scar with a single lick and capture the shame of it between her teeth.

"What troubles you?" Medusa murmured. With that hypnotic mouth so close, she felt the words more than hearing them.

"I want the stitching out." Anger wrenched through the fear in Petra's heart, twisting her speech into a snarl. "I'll cut my tongue open again myself if I have to."

"Don't be ridiculous." The gorgon pulled back just enough for Petra to see green eyes narrow in consideration. "Let me go and I'll do it properly."

Were it anyone else, the offer would have read as a ploy. Who wouldn't take advantage, when she had left her weakness open for a stranger's blade to stab deep and carve out? But Medusa could have wounded her in a thousand other ways, less sacred, less personal. Sadism afforded no inherent leverage.

Petra relaxed her hold around the gorgon. The nest of serpents atop Medusa's head remained sedate, falling back to emerald-accented shoulders, and once both legs were free, her re-action was little more than a sigh. Petra expected the other woman to rise and seek a knife—or whatever else happened to be sharp and in reach—but Medusa turned to face her instead, breast to breast, and cupped the basilisk's face between both hands.

Their second kiss was twice as fierce, a devouring by any other name. Petra moaned as her jaw was forced open, lacquered nails slicing into her cheeks, urging her teeth even farther apart. Full-fledged fangs scraped her bottom lip, and a hard push pinned Petra's head against the floor.

Then Medusa bit straight through her tongue.

Blood poured into Petra's mouth, held in her throat like a chalice. Pain was secondary to sheer surprise as one of Medusa's canines hooked on her prize and pulled, ripping flesh asunder. She jerked back from Petra's face, mouth and chin dripping crimson, then turned and spit out a ragged red thread. It was a fossilized, fetid thing, years of bondage trapped in its ragged weave.

Elation outpaced agony as the fork of Petra's tongue healed—properly, this time—and she swallowed past the taste of hot copper. Words of gratitude didn't seem like enough. She leaned upward and tested her new freedom with a swift lick over Medusa's chin, capturing scent and taste in a single gesture. Another flick made the gorgon shiver, so Petra put her all into the momentary worship, carefully cleaning her essence from black and green scales.

"You're mad," Petra whispered as she finished. "A knife would have been much easier."

"And I would have savored it far less," Medusa said, nonplussed. "One ambush deserves another, after the way you found me here."

The mercenary's chest rumbled with laughter. "Some ambush. I didn't plan on arriving here naked and half-armed."

"Saved me the trouble of stripping you." One red nail traced past the pulse in Petra's neck, following the heat beneath her skin to where the strap of the scabbard cut a diagonal from shoulder to hip. "Shall I rid you of this as well?"

"Only if you give my fangs back in exchange," Petra said, then flashed the filed-down tragedy of her teeth. "One punch would probably do the trick."

"Now who's gone mad?" Medusa muttered, even as she readjusted her weight, settling her hips over Petra's. "Take care, basilisk. I'm starting to suspect you're enjoying this."

Petra smirked. "What I'll enjoy is biting you as hard as you bit me."

The gorgon's fist was a chisel meeting marble. The curse that would have left Petra's mouth was replaced with teeth knocked loose, and several simply shattered. She spat out the remnants before the jagged edges could wound her already sensitive lips even further, grimacing as raw roots joined to new bone. New and visceral, with points capable of piercing steel or crushing a man's femur into dust. As she ran her tongue over the tips, testing their razor's edge, Petra's smile reemerged, flush with predatory joy. Who needed a crown upon the head when she could rule with these alone?

"I'm tempted to apologize for the state of your floor," Petra said.

Medusa leaned back and stretched, exposing the line of her throat; the perfect place to drape a necklace of bruises, whether with grasping hands or seizing jaws. "Don't. By the time I have what I want, Poseidon himself won't be able to wash this stone clean."

Another surge coursed through Petra's stomach before splitting in two. Slickness gathered at the tapered slit between her thighs, hidden by a subtle fold of scales. Were Medusa to slide an inch lower, she would surely feel the rising heat, eager to slip loose. Petra rested her hands on the outside of the gorgon's thighs and squeezed; she needed to steady herself before arousal got the better of her.

"And what is it that you want?"

"Well..." Medusa reached for the strained pin at her shoulder, then drew the metal needle free with one delicate squeeze. "...first things first."

The chiton unraveled, baring the other swell of her breast as the cloth fell, forming a soft black ring around exquisite hips. Petra's impulse to rip the garment away and expose Medusa completely was waylaid by those similarly exquisite hands capturing the fabric and sweeping it from a shell-pink stomach to the pale curves above. She drew the linen like a sash over Petra's collarbones, but when the length draped across shining black eyes, the basilisk shivered and seized Medusa's wrists in an iron grip.

"I have been unable to see for long enough," Petra hissed.

Rather than fight, the other woman let her makeshift blindfold go slack. When their gazes met again, wariness creased Medusa's brow. "Did they take your sight from you too?"

"A single look kills, same as yours. I had no choice but to hide it." After relaxing her hold, Petra found purchase on Medusa's thighs again, thumbs drawing circles over the oblong scales guarding each knee. "But even if that wasn't true, I won't be denied the pleasure of observing your body as it was meant to be."

And said pleasure was unmatched. Cords of muscle tapered up Medusa's legs to the flare of her waist, where green scales blossomed up the length of her belly, deepening in shade toward the gorgon's ribs and lower still. At the shadowed apex of her thighs, she was soft and unarmored, a hint of blood-reddened arousal peeking forth.

Petra wanted to slip inside her and paint that color wide in one rough stroke. She wanted to take the subtle glory of Medusa's breasts into her mouth and pull the dark caps of each nipple between her teeth until they hardened against her tongue. To worship every inch of the scales before her until they shone like aventurine and hematite under the morning sky. For the gorgon was so clearly a woman meant to be seen in the light, yet had been forced from sight time and again. Petra imagined their limbs entwined, so close they interlocked into a mosaic, colors bleeding into one another, both border and boundless.

If Medusa thrashed and fought, all the better. Her venom was sweet and potent as a seer's brew. It would be sweeter still, Petra thought, if the gorgon's fangs sank in while she rode the edge of release, one holy emission spilling into another. She rarely desired—much less allowed—another woman to breach her body in any way, but Medusa provided a temptation like no other, an ouroboros of bliss in the making, if they both dared to bite down.

Yet nothing would happen if she didn't act.

Petra surged upward to claim another kiss, spine unfurling with a ripple of ardor, her insistent sent grip keeping the gorgon confined to her lap. That hot and seeking hunger was answered with fangs, tongue, and a moan which vibrated through Petra's ears, radiating out over her skull like a brush of palms from crest to nape. She didn't resist when Medusa worked the clasp of her scabbard open, parting one strap from another until the xiphos fell from her back and struck the floor. The weight no longer mattered, not with Petra's natural armory made anew, keen to whet other blades against the gorgon's flesh.

In a way, this truly was like the palaestra, reading body language and intent, the move ahead of the move. Supremacy wouldn't be found in a sudden throw or choke, but in pursuing Medusa's pleasure, until arousal outpaced intuition. Ecstasy could forge beautiful weapons when the heat of every nerve was stoked beyond reckoning.

Petra pushed one thigh up between Medusa's legs, smearing her essence across pale scales, polish on marble. The gorgon's back arched, a bow demanding an huntress' grip, and found it when Petra pulled the other woman down, urging Medusa to spread herself and grind.

"How long has it been?" the basilisk asked.

"Since this came from someone I wanted?" Green eyes darkened to nightshade; old pains, old poison. "An eternity."

Before Petra could dowse the depths behind those words, Medusa's hand plunged past the tangle of their limbs, seeking a need to match her own. She found it in the sensitive vent where Petra's scales parted, glistening, promising a treasure just out of reach. Petra muffled a groan into the curve of Medusa's neck, then refocused her efforts with a slow scrape of fangs downward. When her lips found a nipple, fruit-soft against her tongue, Petra captured the whole of it in her mouth and sucked. Medusa's other hand seized, driving lacquered nails into the curve of Petra's hip; they both gasped.

She broke the seal of her mouth with a sharp, wet sound. Medusa's nipple was hard and dark as a seed now, the bloom of blood just beneath the surface. "Does this please you?"

"Have I somehow made myself unclear?" The hand at Petra's hip sought to guide her head instead, dragging parted lips to the gorgon's other breast. "Or are you the sort who needs a woman screaming to believe her in ecstasy?"

Petra laughed, the sound muffled, but a hard twinge pulled high in her chest. "No. But it's like singing a poem and praying the meaning falls well on another's ears. I can only guess."

She was about to occupy herself once more, tongue darting out to draw a circle of heat around the obsidian areola, when Medusa yanked her head back. Petra hissed, denied her prize, only to quiet at the portentous look on the gorgon's face.

"Has no one ever done as such to you?" Medusa asked.

Petra had always wondered what it felt like when she fed from another's breast, a curiosity threaded through dozens of lovers who spent the night in her lap. Some had tips so tender even a faint rasp of teeth was too much to bear, while others yearned to be treated like a wineskin, as if they could be drunk to the last drop by a lover with thirst to spare. She thought there was little point in asking for the favor to be returned before, but now that Agnodice's potion ran through her veins, a yearning long out of reach suddenly felt close enough to taste.

The basilisk's throat went dry. "There is not enough to…"

"There is more than enough."

A huff followed, one Petra mistook as dismissal until Medusa slipped down her body, impatient—eager. Nestled between alabaster scales was a budding softness, and the gorgon kissed the shell-pink tip of it, lips parted, tongue gloriously hot. Petra's knee jerked, forcing her leg higher between straining thighs, and the short cry that erupted from the other woman's throat sent a vibrating shock through Petra's entire body. It was as if new nerves were being woven into place under Medusa's mouth, threads which tied themselves deep into the basilisk's heart, burning away doubt and leaving behind unvarnished pleasure.

Every forked caress roused a different feeling: flickers of friction, liquid heat quenched into aching arousal, the dual brush of being memorized as the gorgon moved from breast to breast. Petra needed another anchor to buoy herself through the shifting waves of sensation, and drew a hand up Medusa's back until her fingers were buried in the nest of serpents resting atop the gorgon's head. Her presence was welcomed; a dozen writhing bodies the color of volcanic jasper, split green and swallowing black, slipped around and between Petra's fingers, drawing her digits in like a mating ball, searching for an opening.

The world collapsed to points of heat. She no longer saw the chamber or the godly artifacts—even her own sword had slipped from view—only brutal flashes of color as she found a rhythm with the firm, fast slide of her thigh against Medusa's dripping folds and the red, faceted gem of her clit, free from its setting, hood pulled back. The gorgon's mouth felt like a golden ring around Petra's nipples, drawn tight over and over again, luring sensitive flesh out into the open until no one could ignore their glorious shape. In tandem, green-ridged knuckles drew a cunning circle around Petra's slit, as if silently asking the pouch within to open.

She couldn't resist. Every wall built for control, secured to a foundation of denial, was crumbling away. Petra had run countless lovers through this maze, leading them to dead ends designed to pass power back into her hands. Humans didn't know any better, so caught up in the need to please that they never considered what lay past the stone, mere inches out of reach. Why would they dig deeper? She rewarded their ignorance with as much bliss as could be unleashed upon a body while leaving mortal flesh intact.

Lay back, surrender, close your eyes. The monster can't kill if its gaze isn't met directly. Yet to look away was to deny more than her stare.

Petra gasped as one dripping, pink length emerged from her slit and pushed into Medusa's questing hand. It was blood-heavy as the other woman's clit, the same fusion of flesh but with a tapered tip, decorated with eager opalescence. She filled the gorgon's fingers, enough to squeeze and stroke. Agnodice's work had freed her of the weight underneath, and a torment of the past was washed away, drowned in sudden relief, a crashing wave of joy. Revelation stole Petra's speech; she could only moan and pray the sound translated.

When Medusa looked up, lips parted, her mirth was mirrored, but further in that reflection was reverent lust and the open wonder of glorious discovery. She allowed her hand to open, glancing down as Petra's soft weight draped to the left. Carmine nails traced invisible lines along her clit, mapping her as familiar territory.

"How pretty," Medusa said. "Although I thought your kind always had two."

Surprise—and no small amount of pride—unfurled in Petra's breast before she answered, low and wry, "Most women cannot handle two. Whether divided or both at once."

The gorgon's hold subtly constricted; a hot throb of pleasure punctured Petra's belly, wide and deep as a spear. "Do you look upon me and see a woman like any other, basilisk? I would have all of you. As much as I can take."

Her point came emphasized with a renewed grind of gracile hips, painting another opaque streak of arousal down Petra's thigh. Absent hesitation or interrogation, it was a bid to continue and find out what else their bodies shared.

No, Medusa was not a woman like any other, singular in form as one could be. It was an ultimatum she set upon the world, an unshakable persistence despite every inch of flesh that had been transmuted against her will. Yes, *and*. A monster, *too*. The truth could not be culled from her, whether by the gods or mortal folly.

Yet her breed was one Petra knew across nations: a woman for women, half of a puzzle seeking its interlocking piece. A piece she had also carried her entire life, never a man but holding a certain essence oft mistaken as one and the same. Her similar pursuits did not mean she possessed the same consumptive drives, no matter how often such poison had been dribbled in her ear.

The polis was a spiked collar around every citizen's neck, flaunted like jewelry while blood drenched every step they took. It would have her reshape Medusa into a wife, tallied above a slave but below the yearly tithe of grain. In human demesnes, land and ownership created men; those who did not possess a stretch of ground and the people upon it could scarcely be called a man at all. To rebuke the notion was to be branded a traitor, damned further than those who were never granted honor to begin with.

Petra owned nothing, save herself. She had partitioned her body for so long—trading some pieces, hiding others—in exchanges that could be called violence, but she fought to name them freedom. How much death could a stolen glance buy, or her chosen name on a priestess' lips? A nation's worth, on certain days. If Medusa wanted all of her, she could have everything from head to toe.

"Keep stroking, then," Petra rasped, "and perhaps you'll earn it."

The gorgon laughed. One heraldic note, triumphant, echoing to the pinnacle of the mountain. Challenge and victory both, so bright that the gleam spilled from her eyes to the whole of her face. "Gladly."

They clashed again, a chiaroscuro of shifting limbs. Petra dictated the pace of Medusa's ever-rolling hips, keeping a constant cycle of friction between the swollen petals of her cunt and scale-bound strength. The angle of the basilisk's thigh sharpened every time Medusa plied her for a kiss, fangs snapping at one another, more wolf than serpent. She tightened her grip in the venomous nest of snakes, forcing out a chorus of gasps, loud enough to mask her own moan as Medusa chased her clit with eager pulls from base to tip. So much slickness was smeared and mingled across shared skin, it became impossible to tell where the headwaters began.

"Look at you trembling," Petra said. "One touch to that little ruby between your legs and I think you would—"

Medusa's fingers plunged low, toying with the gossamer-like membrane just beyond Petra's slit, and the last word perished in her throat.

"That I would what, king of serpents?" Another subtle thrust, two mere digits, but within, further than anyone else had ever tried to go. "Shatter?"

Such a small gap, and yet Petra could not think past the sensation as

Medusa delved into the sleek opening, treating the space where her clit branched from left to right like something worthy of exploration on its own. There was an inexplicable sense of danger—*fragility*—when soft fingertips and lacquer-cast nails joined together and curled, finding a spot that felt like a knot of warm silk, as if she could be unraveled and exposed with a single moment of pressure.

Other women had ridden Petra, taken her into their throats, begged to be thrown down and mounted past the point of endurance. Pleasure could be found in such games when the mood suited her, but with the act came other expectations. An austere sort of hardness, draining body and soul until she became rigid from lack of feeling. She was inclined to dominance, to offering protection, yet even a shield was meant to be held close; a shield should be rightfully cared for after the battle was done.

Medusa was the first in so long to push past that, to search for what might have lay inside her from the very beginning. Something waiting for curiosity, for care. Petra let the bliss of it wash over her, welcoming the gorgon's hand by folding her unoccupied knee down against the floor, hips opened like an offering.

"We'll both break," she declared. "It's only a matter of who collapses last."

Before Medusa could answer, Petra raked her nails across the speckled green band of one hip, cutting a curve around the firm contour of the other woman's ass before her fingers dug in too, squeezing hard. The snarled curse that followed only urged Petra on—she didn't have to be inside Medusa to feel the full-body clench rippling through every limb—quickening the drag and thrust of her thigh, never breaking contact with the gorgon's dripping cunt or the twitching, sanguine swell of her clit.

Vengeance came with another long stroke up her own length. Medusa's rhythm was calculated, dipping her fingers in the well of Petra's slit and returning drenched, drawing that gloss to the very tip where pearls of need spilled forth and trickled back down. Wetness in service of wetness, seeking to ruin Petra in the flood. There was no friction to stop the right branch of her clit from slipping loose and narrowing the gap between the pair, turning each exploratory dive of Medusa's hand into a lingering, almost virginal stretch.

Ecstasy spun hot and endless coils through Petra's gut, threading through one another until she wasn't sure if she wanted to arch back, buck her hips, or simply howl herself hoarse. Medusa moaned between staggered breaths, writhing in the basilisk's lap. Their brows were pressed together, balancing one another against the inevitable fall. A new tremor arose in Medusa's hips, short and quick, and it was a quivering Petra knew so very well, a body held right above the topple of release.

Then two sets of fangs sank into the basilisk's wrist. Flanking the pulse, inundating her veins with a double dose of venom. Victory was seized by tiny, dueling jaws as Petra's blood ignited in a single white-hot burst of pleasure, swept away by orgasm from one breath to the next. The slow and steady drip from her clits spasmed into a sudden deluge, essence overflowing until Medusa's hand was coated to the wrist.

Bliss blotted out higher thought. Ambition boiled down to a thick, primal haze. It was as if her entire body had turned into a thin-walled vessel, meant to hold nothing but liquid heat. Every shudder of Petra's limbs sent the feeling splashing up to her breast, into her throat. She wasn't sure where her flesh ended and the gorgon's began until aching lungs offered a reminder to breathe, and the silver wash across Petra's vision opened into glittering gaps, revealing the woman who had conquered her so effortlessly.

Medusa, shoulders high and proud, knees shamelessly spread. Medusa, whose eyes blazed with triumph but whose mouth was parted and glistening with need. Those fang-stung lips began to form words—be it her name or a goad, who knew—but Petra refused to leave her half of the challenge unanswered.

She interrupted with a kiss, a claim enkindled, a brand forced past the teeth and pressed straight to the tongue. Momentum reversed their positions, putting Medusa on her back against the marble, unable to twist loose or roll away with the demanding presence of Petra's thigh between her legs. They landed together with breathless impact, a desperate cry pushed from the gorgon's lungs as Petra rutted against the other woman's cunt in hard, deep strokes.

One hand ensnared Medusa's throat, squeezing above the verdigris crest of her collarbones, and the other sought the monuments across her body: nipples swollen like beads of onyx, only to give under Petra's fingers like clay, prelude to the drag of nails along a supple stomach, the dip and rise from hip to hip, and finally the full, aching jewel of Medusa's clit. She was almost too wet to touch, slipping against the basilisk's fingertips until Petra trapped its length between the V of her digits and applied brusque circles with her thumb. There was no pause to breathe or beg, only a relentless, commanding rhythm, caught between the grind of her thigh and an utterly focused hand.

The shattering was sweet. Petra swallowed Medusa's scream as it vibrated against her palm and spilled into her mouth, a shout of warning before the gorgon thrashed and tumbled over the edge, sinuous hips losing their grace, falling into broken, jagged movements. No longer a performance but raw, animal need—ravenous. Pleasure tore into her, leaving Medusa's body slack and blood-flush by the end, the glass of her eyes so dulled by ecstasy that it could be mistaken for death, were not her chest snapping upward and seeking greedy gulps of air.

Petra loomed above Medusa in the afterglow, hands still but cradling the pulses of groin and throat like they might escape the flesh above with their wardrum beats. Breath by breath, the rhythm slowed, and with that echo gone, Petra heard their mixed fluids dripping past spent limbs and down onto the marble. The perfume cast throughout the chamber had been over-run by a miasma of musk and ichor, the incense of beasts.

"You fell first," Medusa whispered, the greater volume of her voice still locked away.

When Petra smiled, it bared the full extent of her fangs. "But not alone. Should we measure the distance togeth-er? The depth?"

Another laugh, dry but warm, left the gorgon's throat. Petra wanted to roll around in the sound until it coated her like pankration oil. "You have even greater *depths* than expected, basilisk."

She could only watch—in hunger, in awe—as Medusa reached down to gath-er a drop of iridescent essence from the left branch of her clit, soft and half-re-tracted. When the gorgon brought that finger to her lips and the fork of her tongue flickered out, the sound that followed was one of unambiguous curiosity.

"And another riddle here," Medusa said. "What is different?"

"I spill only for pleasure now," Petra admitted, eyes still locked on her own arousal, coating Medusa's finger like a ring. "That was the bargain I made with Cybele's chosen, that my seed would no longer take root. That the alchemy of my body would change."

It was a comfort, if anything, that the other woman could already tell. Petra trusted Agnodice's expertise, but better to be sure before spilling herself inside another. Breeding was a tumultuous, complicated fantasy, but she was free to toy with such desires now, absent consequence.

"So noted. The taste is sweeter," Medusa added wryly. "But have I answered your question, Petra?"

"In part." Afterglow usually carried exhaustion in its wake; this time, Petra felt reinvigorated, as if the fading heat in her limbs would only need a single touch to stir again. "Is there anything you want to ask in return?"

"My fear is we are too alike by far." The gorgon's words were punctuated by a light push to Petra's shoulders, breaking the line between their bodies as she eased away. "Will you fight me for every inch of new ground we discover together?"

Petra knew a question loaded with lead shot when she heard one. "I won't surrender unequivocally, if that's what you mean. But I don't think you would either."

"Never." Medusa's smile carried more venom than the snakes upon her head. "But I prefer to hunt the willing, when I'm given the chance."

As the other woman rose to her feet, Petra did the same, languor unfurling through her stomach and dispelling the weary ache of long-bent knees. Medusa turned to open the wooden chest at the foot of her bed, and the basilisk forgot entirely about what danger could lay in wait as the gorgon's back was revealed to her.

Hexagonal black scales guarded each vertebrae like armor, but the subtle triangular divots between them were the color of prasinon, sharp sprouts of spring waiting to pierce somber earth. The base of Medusa's spine ended on another finial of green, tapering outward to frame her flanks, only to come together at the backs of each thigh, a heart shape dividing sculpted hamstrings from the trim shape of her rear. There the darker scales were small and smooth; Petra knew that from touch alone. No tail, of course, but she couldn't judge the lack after casting her own aside.

"Your gaze does more than kill, it seems." The gorgon's voice snapped Petra's attention upward—not to Medusa's mouth, but the subtle glint of metal in one hand. "Look as you like, but clean yourself up, too, before our coupling dries."

Medusa tossed the implement toward her as if it were a blade, but when Petra captured the flash of silver out of midair, a stlegis stood out between her fingers. The angular design could have been found in a thousand bathhouses and gymnasia, its metal curved to drag and capture oil from the skin. Yet she could tell it was a well-loved instrument, polished up to the handle without a scratch to be seen. Chances were, Medusa had never used it on any other body but her own.

"You're sure?" Petra asked, trying to hide her trepidation, the sudden implication of intimacy.

"Had you human skin instead of scales, I might be more particular," the gorgon said, now on one knee, buried above the shoulders in the depths of the chest. Whatever she sought had not been needed in quite some time. "But yes, I'm sure."

Petra braced the silver edge against her leg and wicked it upward in a slow, repeating pattern, leaving nothing but the natural sheen of her own hide behind. Feeling clean was its own novelty now that she'd shed again, washing herself directly rather than through the discomfort of a veil. Were she not so newly stripped, Petra could have spent an hour polishing herself from head to toe and reveling in such luxury of sensation.

But when she looked up again, the object in Medusa's hand was of far greater interest. Braids of russet leather formed a harness around an—Petra weighed several descriptors in her mind and settled on "aspirational"—phallus, made of a similarly ruddy, high quality hide. There was true weight to the length and not a seam or stitch to be found, the sort of detailed work usually ascribed to cordwainers fitting noble sandals, or cuirasses of decorative armor gifted to temples.

"Don't tell me you had those wide-eyed fisherfolk import that from the mainland for you," Petra said.

Medusa clicked her tongue in open annoyance. "Please. I made this myself, from tanning and dye to the wax mold for a proper shape. They sent me raw hides and brass for the fittings, nothing more."

"And this occupied you under the earth, all alone?"

"Craft keeps the mind sharp," the gorgon countered. "Leather, especially. When it comes to materials, a second skin is temperamental. More than most."

A few clever comments rose to Petra's tongue, but arguing that particular point was doomed to make her look foolish. "So when you spent hours shaping such a fine and heavy cock under your hands, were you imagining someone would arrive to use it on you?"

Facets of defiance honed green eyes once more, whetted edges striking against desire with the ease of pyrite and iron. "Far from it. I was imagining a naive little thing, lost and seeking succor, being spread under my hands and then mounted until she wept."

That desire turned outward, knife-like, and scraped a hot line along Petra's stomach. Such a thing was simple to picture: the harness snug against the framing arrows of Medusa's hips, one hand idly stroking the phallus between them as she considered exactly how to rend some doe-eyed maiden beneath her asunder. Yet the basilisk had never been allowed to be the sort of girl swept away in such innocent fantasies;

they demanded a purity held outside of her reach.

"But dreams are meaningless on their own," Medusa continued. "Why would I focus on some ephemeral endeavor when I could be sharing my lust with the alluring, handsome woman before me right now?"

The knife sunk deeper and twisted, threatening to spill Petra's viscera in a crimson maze across the floor. How long had it been since someone called her "handsome" in the right way, with purpose and not mistaken intent? She could count the simple compliment across the ages on one hand, almost two, but a different tenor emerged when certain women uttered the word—an understanding which could not be captured or copied.

"Perhaps we can come to an agreement." Petra strung each word together with care, coaxing out a balance between force and surrender. "But your fingers, lovely as they were, barely managed to fit. Your toy would struggle to even start."

"Well, that depends on where it goes, doesn't it?" Medusa let the harness hang between her fingers like the top of a sling and stepped forward, free hand closing the distance to grab the swell of Petra's ass and squeeze. Carmine nails drew invisible circles over one cheek before pressing toward the cleft, applying enough pressure to part the basilisk open, just so. "My cock would fit perfectly here, I think. Maybe that and more."

Petra had only done such an act once before, during yet another pointless campaign between Athens and Sparta. Mercenaries were being snapped up by the highest bidder, and several regiments changed sides at the last minute, carving trenches of tension through what neutral tents remained. It was the worst place to meet a woman like herself—mortal, but otherwise the same—especially when the opposing commanders began to offer wine and other vices to sweeten their offers. Intoxication was Dionysus' trade, and he plied it in full, whipping a frenzy throughout the camp.

Antheia came from Crete, expertise forged in battles along the Aegean coast. Petra only heard her name a single time, whispered in the dead of night when they found one another, away from the ring of fire where bribe after bribe had collapsed into brutal festivity. Under moonlight, Antheia's black hair was threaded through with silver, her luxurious brown eyes carrying the stars. She had a phial of oil and an offer, couched in gentle words which would have been easy to overlook, if the listener deemed her a threat to one's pride. Well-practiced, burned before.

A pain wholly undeserved.

And a pain Petra felt compelled to soothe, even if she could only do so in the dark, armor half undone. Antheia accepted a claim of inexperience with aplomb, assuming it was one of many firsts, knowing nothing of the immortal she took to bed. Few words were exchanged, but her kindness bled through every syllable, soaking into murmurs of quiet praise. The humiliation Petra had been told in no uncertain words to expect never arrived.

They both accepted contracts the next morning—by some mercy, to the same army—but never spoke of what happened again. Petra sensed a primal fear from Antheia if she lingered too close during meals or drills, as if proximity to one another risked exposure to everyone else. Her own lineage lessened such consequence, but any other woman trapped among thousands of soldiers would have had nowhere to run, so Petra swallowed the agony of maintaining her distance until victory separated them, coin pouches filled and pushed in opposing directions.

But here, in the now, Medusa was less a kindred spirit and more a kindred force, demanding that whatever energy was spent found its enthusiastic echo. Petra's eyes did a slow, purposeful sweep over the phallus the gorgon held, gauging its well-crafted width, how far the length of oiled leather would push inside her and claim.

"I could be convinced..." The basilisk's gaze flickered upward, seeking its lethal twin. "...if you let me do the same to you."

A cunning, cutting sound erupted from Medusa's throat, closer to a bark than a laugh. "Ah, so we're bargaining now."

"No bargain," Petra countered. "If I give you the chance to ruin me, I should be allowed to return the favor. It's only fair."

"And I am the very pinnacle of fairness and justice." Amusement underlined Medusa's voice with a rasp. "Athena herself weeps to look upon me."

That was probably true, Petra reasoned, if not for the reasons implied.

She broke the distance between them with a single step, barricading Medusa in against a corner of the chamber. Not as an impassable wall, but a gate of temptation, ready to open with the right signal. Then she leaned down to meet the other woman's ear, the heat of her breath rustling the wary nest of serpents surrounding that slender shell, and whispered: "I think you want to bury your cock inside me so badly, you'd risk me tearing you apart afterward. How about that?"

Medusa went taut as a string under a lyrist's fingertip, breath held and waiting to be plucked free. Petra refused to relent, pressed close and unblinking, until the hand at her back quivered and gave away the answer to come.

"Yes," Medusa said. "I would risk that and more."

"Then let us put that bed of yours to good use." Petra straightened to her full height again, wielding an insouciant grin. "I won't let you shatter my knees plowing me into a floor made out of obsidian."

"I can have your teeth and your tongue, but not your knees?" The gorgon mused as Petra took a step back. "Do you have some secret weakness there, like darling Achilles?"

"Achilles would accost you with far more grace than I," Petra countered. "Such is a heroine's nature."

"Then it is a good thing I have no want for grace, is it not?" A bold thing to say, the basilisk thought, as she watched Medusa step into the bounds of the harness like she had done so a thousand times before, pairing red-hued leather to the crimson vault between her legs. "Only a serpent like myself will do."

And said serpent sat upon the abyssal silk of the gorgon's bed, dyed so dark Petra could taste the tannins and iron flooding the fabric, the latter scent holding a tang like fresh blood. She had sprawled on klines and slept on wooden racks full of woven reeds, but most nights were spent with the leather she carried tucked underneath her head, surrounded by whatever stretch of canvas survived league after league of travel. Medusa's bed was a throne stretched to excess, its frame of olive wood and ivory curling upward at the end as a high wave of a headboard, upon which an ouroboros was carved intaglio, the shadows between each subtle cut high-lighting a closed loop of scales.

Petra did not ask whose hand had wrought it into being. Who else stood at the bottom of an endless well of time? Who else would flake and scour her pain into something so beautiful, even knowing such a masterpiece might never be seen by another?

The basilisk's knuckles scraped against the sheets. A single shedding could not smooth a life of combat from hands skilled in sword and spear, shield and fist. The silk was tempting in its own way, soft and unsullied, asking for a cruel grip. One curious rake of her hand sent ripples outward across the bed, sure as a rock plunged into the sea.

"Tear that and I'll use your hide to replace it," Medusa warned. "Besides, I want you on your stomach, basilisk."

When Petra's eyes narrowed—she was no camp follower, paid to be faceless—the other woman smiled and leaned close. "Do I not get to savor your back the way you savored mine? You are a peak that must be climbed from both sides."

It was a clever, manipulative comment, but her mood leaned more clay than stone in the moment, eager for the shaping. Petra brought the rest of her body onto the bed, unambiguously pleased when the luxurious frame welcomed her from head to toe, and settled onto all fours. She stretched her arms to their limit, head bowed like a lioness in repose, and from behind Medusa's breath staggered, coming to a halt in that noble throat. Face obscured by the scaffold of her shoulders, Petra could not help but grin.

"Your gaze does more than kill, too, I see." She glanced back, just enough to see Medusa's pupils blown wide, the green of her eyes diminished to a sliver. "But it can't fuck me, so you'll have to do the deed yourself."

"I'm in no rush," the gorgon hissed back, even as she reached into the chest once more, procuring a lekythos of oil with impressive haste. The capped white-figure pot had two nymphs etched upon it, their coupling shrouded by the trunk of an olive-laden tree. "Fairness may not be one of my virtues, but patience certainly is."

Petra had every intention of putting that patience to the test. She let her attention fall back to the headboard and its myriad coils, pale as her own, and sunk an inch further into the surrounding dark. The bed dipped behind her as Medusa's weight settled, knee over knee, and red-veiled nails found the fine arch of Petra's hips. Contact was brief, the pass of an artisan weighing new material and picturing the creation to be found therein.

Warm green palms slid higher, framing the solitaire scales on either side of Petra's spine that led to both shoulders, the statuesque line of her neck. When Medusa reached the light pink pattern sheathing her throat, that lacquered touch sank in, forming an anchor before the other woman lay flush against her back. The weight was easy to bear but undeniable, especially when the substantial bulge of Medusa's shaft followed suit, its promise lingering in every hot inch against Petra's skin. Such was one of the many benefits of leather: it conducted heat, it drank and wore oil like any other flesh.

Medusa's next words were uttered right against the basilisk's ear. "And that patience means I will bide my time until the moment that you break. No matter how long that takes. No matter how many times I must stamp my claim inside that swift-healing body of yours."

A firm push urged Petra's face to the sheets, and the next thing she heard was the ceramic cap of the lekythos being pried open. The faint tang of oil became a flood, pouring past Petra's nose and tongue, its scent coating every breath on the way down to her lungs. Liquid gold from Lesbos—there was no greater olive grove to be found in Greece—alloyed with the faint mist of foam from the sea, carried from hand to treasuring hand, held like a breath inside its vessel of wax and clay.

When a gold-slick digit pressed against the tight ring of muscle above Petra's slit, she braced for a sharp intrusion, but it was Medusa's folded knuckle that sank inside her with ease, not the crimson flare of her nails. A gratifying ache answered the calculating stretch, and Petra choked back a gasp, determined to hold her tongue as long as she could. What joy was there for either of them if she surrendered so easily?

"So this is where the rest of your color is hiding," Medusa declared as she worked a second bent finger in besides the first. When her knuckles parted, spreading Petra open, a hiss slipped past grit teeth. "Pink as the bed of Aphrodite's shell. And red if I dare deep enough, I'm sure."

Somehow the third slipped into her the easiest, as if waiting for the true test, and when Medusa pumped her fingers in an exploratory thrust, pleasure spun in a searing coil up Petra's spine, each loop wound tighter than the next. Her hands clenched into fists against the sheets, out of sight beside her head—or so Petra thought before the susurrating chorus of Medusa's laugh met the air, her amusement echoed by dozens of narrow serpentine throats.

"Don't bother to stifle your pleasure, Petra." Medusa's fingers withdrew as a trio, leaving Petra aching, *empty*. "You need not say a word when the truth lies written in the glory of your body. Every detail is... magnified."

Any answer she might have given as wit or protest vanished when the head of Medusa's cock pressed against her, its thick tip dripping but no less formidable. The pressure transformed into a deep stretch with the subtle tilt of lithe hips, urging the first heady inch inside.

"And full of spoils aplenty," the gorgon added breathlessly.

She went slow. Petra would have called the pace sedate were it not such a blatant goad, keeping her in place like a dazed insect, pinned and fluttering under the fingertip of a fascinated observer. Any hint of agony would have bolstered her defenses, turning this into a trial of endurance instead of a constant temptation to rock her hips back and take the rest of Medusa's shaft hilt-deep. Instead, Petra could only bow her head against the banner of black below as she was opened like an animal on an altar, the gorgon's ritualistic rhythm masquerading as mercy.

"Should I remind you to breathe?" Medusa asked, knuckles kneading circles into a knot of tension near Petra's waist. "There's such a gorgeous flush spreading down your back."

Petra's exhale was forceful, loud with intent. "You want more than my breath."

"Absolutely." She was more than halfway now, by Petra's measure, but showed no signs of either reticence or haste, balanced on the torturous edge in between. "Will you give it to me?"

"I won't beg, queen of serpents." Petra took a certain visceral joy in reshaping the title that had lured her half a dozen times over. "Either conquer me or retreat."

A hand gripped the nape of her neck and squeezed. "This is more of a siege, is it not?"

So it was, until the building pressure inside Petra became a demanding fullness, far enough to send a ripple of need through her gut. Medusa's first thrust was shallow, another test, but the next had the directed vigor of a battering ram. The shift in strength came so abrupt and absolute that a moan slipped past the line of Petra's sealed lips, and once one sound had left her, a hundred others were determined to follow suit.

Yet Medusa's tempo never lapsed into a thoughtless, maladroit rut, every rough plunge within countered by her meticulous withdrawal. There was a hint of leniency in the movements, as if Petra might be allowed to recover each time the gorgon pulled back, but it was never quite long enough, racing the beat of her heart and winning by a blink time and again. Even with both hands by the headboard, a welcoming jolt traveled through her slit and the branches of her clits started to swell. Their rousing was faster than the first time, almost habitual, like when she touched herself, grinding against whatever forgiving surface she could straddle.

"And what is this upon your back?" Medusa asked, voice free of exertion, even as her cock maintained its ceaseless rhythm. "One last gift you've kept from me."

Petra frowned. "What are you—"

Her demand stalled the instant Medusa's nails scraped over the oval-shaped scar at the base of her spine. After shedding, the edges were more subtle, its surface smooth as temple tile, but that made the old wound impossible to miss without the division of scales for camouflage. Sensation dulled there, a void when compared to the rest of her nerves, which sang like kithara strings under the gorgon's provocative touch.

Yet Medusa's hand lingered, fingers parting to measure the whole of Petra's loss, grasping what was no longer there. "You told me your tail had been severed. Was it here?"

Petra squeezed her eyes shut, as if forsaking her vision would veil the truth, making what had happened easier to bear. "Yes."

"Why didn't it grow again?"

Because she had used the hottest metal she could find to cauterize what desperate vestige remained, killing her body's impulse to grow, to balance, to be free. Everything had changed as a result: her posture, the tilt of her hips, the ability to detect what was behind her without so much as a glance. Humans saw tails as the provenance of lesser beasts, not the mantle of royalty, the privilege of another limb, a third hand worthy of decoration and celebration. Petra would never have declared any of her sacrifices easy, but slicing that part of herself away had been the most brutal by far. The last time she wept was beside the pyre burning sacred flesh to ash, praying that a proper ceremony would somehow absolve her of the guilt.

It had not.

"Because I made it so," she finally answered. "Do not ask how."

"What was it like?" Medusa pressed, trading one painful question for a different set. "Was it beautiful? A whip to caution whoever challenged your majesty?"

Had the gorgon mocked her, Petra would have readily accepted the injury of forcing the other woman away, destroying the connection between their bodies. But Medusa's tone was equal parts curiosity and sorrow, trying to find meaning in the middle. She may as well have asked, *how do you live, knowing what they've taken from you?*

"Truly beautiful." Petra confessed, clinging to the flickers of defiance in her heart, a flame that had yet to die out. "As thick around as your thigh, and long enough to wrap around your throat. I could swim like a fish and climb like a vervet. Even the most arrogant of chimeras would be brought low by the sight."

For a few breaths, only silence answered. Even Medusa's hips had stilled, caught mid-thrust, as if pushing forward would signal sadistic overreach and pulling out might be taken as disgust or denial. Then the gorgon's nails sank deeper, warring against the leathery plane of the scar and threatening to break through.

"Do you want it back?" Medusa asked softly.

So soft Petra's heart twisted in her chest, like she had just stopped a javelin from cutting the organ in twain. A tenderness unasked for was more threatening than a thousand misthophoroi armed to the teeth. She almost growled a rejection, demanding for Medusa to fuck her and get on with it, but the flare of rage guttered out before reaching her throat, quenched by a need so powerful

Petra could barely fit her mouth around the word.

"*Yes.*"

The gorgon lay against her once more, sinuous body finding alignment from limb to limb, a cameo inset along its frame. Questing serpents' tongues brushed over Petra's head and neck, capturing her scent before Medusa whispered, "Then beg. Not to me, but for forgiveness. This is your penance."

Her words pierced like a needle through the hundredfold knot of Petra's guilt, and found the well of poison fermenting underneath. Hatred—at the world for what it had done, urged her to inflict upon herself—and a bitter yearning, made even more potent each time she caught her reflection and cast her true desires away. To be who she was in full, a woman of contradictions and triumphs both, ill-fitting in any mold except her own.

How cruel she had been to a girl who didn't know any better back then.

"I..." Petra struggled to put the right phrases together, not out of reticence but a true lack of experience. Throughout her life, she had endured a thousand kinds of pain in complete silence, even when crying out might have stopped the torture sooner. "Do it. Give me back what I threw away."

Medusa's hand remained still. "Do what, Petra?"

"Tear me open." It came easier now, crawling closer to the truth now that some sort of clemency was in sight. "Make me bleed—please."

Hard red nails slipped into the gap between scar tissue and pristine scales, blurring the borders of numbness and pain. "Say that again."

She didn't question what part. Petra knew, down to the bone. "Please!"

The gorgon tore into her. Not as something wild but with long and measured slices like Agnodice's scalpel, unerring, without hesitation. Nerves lay sleeping beneath the scar, dead to the world for so long that the first brush of contact brought unspeakable agony. Petra buried her face in the sheets, silk tethered around her fists, but did not cry out until Medusa broke the stalemate between their bodies and thrust forward. Her rhythm remained calm and collected, stirring pleasure to bolster the basilisk against a rising tide of pain. Salve, not punishment. A cure for when that ancient poison met the air, spilling hot in a taper along Petra's back and down either side of her thighs.

When Medusa had shattered her teeth and split her tongue, the misery was instant, gone by the time Petra realized what happened. This unraveling was excruciating in comparison, clawing through layers of ash to find the fertile field underneath. It lasted long enough for the basilisk to remember the sensation of her tail's crown gripped in one hand and her sword in the other, how the single cut through felt like being beheaded. She had almost slit her own throat in the moments afterward to finish the executioner's work.

In Petra's youth, when she was not alone, growth of one's tail was a sign of maturity and allure. She measured the change day by day, against herself, against others, secretly pleased that such serpentine comeliness came from her body without aid. It had been proof of something, although those words had been out of her reach then, too.

Medusa stripped the old brand away. She seized Petra's hips with blood-soaked hands and dragged her back against the bruising width of that thick cock, again and again. Faster now, hard enough that Petra gasped and moaned every time the other woman bottomed out, head bowed, knees spread in unambiguous surrender.

"Just like a virgin to stain my bed." The gorgon's voice was regal but swathed in hunger; a queen breaking in her consort, riding the line between duty and pleasure. "When you've finished ruining the sheets, I'll have to hang this sheet atop the mountain like a flag so everyone knows what I've done to you."

Petra opened her mouth to confess that she wasn't, that this had been done to her before, but she wanted it to be true. Blood running clean, newly reborn. Her orgasm was akin to drowning, seized by an undertow of bliss, losing sight of herself. There was only a twisting, net-like pleasure pulling her down, down, down. There was only the woman inside of her, holding her body beneath the water. Death waited in the dark flood with an open embrace, shades of black and shades of heat becoming one and the same, calling itself *release*.

The basilisk's next breath broke the surface—staggered, shaking, in need. Petra's vision spun and split into innumerable colors, her head yanked back by a flexed arm around her throat. Medusa's breathing was equally jagged, a captivating mix of exertion and languor, the gorgon's body hot as a sunbeam against the plinth of Petra's back. She didn't understand why until her mind pulled the chaos of sensation into order: where her limbs began and where they ended, where raw and sanguine scales had been unsheathed in white down the full length of her tail.

Her tail, uncoiled with power, was presently wedged underneath Medusa's cock and the bottom of the harness, subtle ridges flush with dripping folds and the gorgon's swollen, oversensitive clit. The limb was as great as the day Petra severed it, stretching out into open air. She tested its responsiveness with a subtle flicker, and her tail answered out of instinct, memory woven back into new muscle, alabaster flesh and delicate bone. Medusa groaned at the movement, as much out of protest as surprise.

"Was that bit of contact enough to make you come?" Petra asked, undeniably amused. "Because the rest of me didn't even touch you."

"Don't play arrogant," the other woman hissed. "You fought me so, only to weep at the end. Lovely as a nymph."

The basilisk blinked, only then making sense of why her sight blurred at the edges. She wiped a cooling trail from one side of her face, heady with salt. It had been so long since she last cried, and tears never came with ease, twisted out of her like a drying tunic. These fell freely from her eyes, the rush of a river past a shattered dam, respite following in the water's wake.

That had never happened before.

"It felt good," Petra admitted. "And take your victory for what it is, gorgon. You're the only one alive who's ever seen my tears."

"What an ephemeral treasure." Medusa's tongue darted up her other damp cheek, capturing a drop before it fell. Petra felt her shiver when she swallowed. "Oh. If I could bottle that, all the ambrosia in Olympus wouldn't be worth the trade."

Her compliment stoked the pool of satisfied heat lingering deep in Petra's belly, threatening to reignite a greater fire. "Are you going to pull out, or was the plan to ride my tail like a horse while drinking your fill?"

A bemused scoff followed, and Medusa pushed away from Petra's back. The shaft slipped out absent pain, followed by an emptiness Petra refused to name. She didn't miss the prudent rise of the gorgon's hips, careful to avoid the ridged tail trapped between her thighs until she could swing one leg over to the opposite half of the bed. Petra rolled onto her side to relieve what pressure remained on her elbows and knees, only to be treated to the view of Medusa's cock, leather shimmering with oil and a subtle embossment of blood. The inside of dappled green thighs were coated in a mirrored sheen of arousal.

She watched as the gorgon shifted to her knees and worked the harness loose, braided straps curling into one another once the tension of her body slipped away. Medusa hung it from one corner of the bed with care—noting she couldn't polish anything while the ma-terial was still wet—and stretched out across the black sheets beside Petra. No handmade pigment or dye could compare to the natural shades of a serpent; Medusa dulled the fabric the moment it came near.

"Petra Kruos." The gorgon's tongue skirted over the careful bridge of her name; a simple mortal fusion, created from necessity. Medusa's tone blunted the harshest edge of each syllable, sweetened them like honey. "After endless curses, the gods finally sent me a true gift: a woman of stone, sculpted by her own hand."

"I came of my own accord," Petra replied, resisting the way Medusa's words threatened to sink into her heart, deeper than nails, deeper than fangs. "Cybele's bargain would have been easy to deny, should I have chosen to."

"To find me," Medusa added, "or rather, your answer."

She could have risen and walked away, or told the other woman to leave her be, demanding an hour's sleep after enduring that brutal gauntlet. Instead, Petra glanced between the idle tangle of their feet, past the edge of the bed, and asked, "What else is in that fearsome chest of yours?"

Medusa's lips pursed, teeth clenching. Through the mesh of green and black framing her cheeks, Petra saw the sudden rush of blood, iridescent lines of heat. Embarrassment, of all things—yet what could embarrass the woman who lay across from her after they had fucked one another like beasts seeking spring?

"Nothing that is your concern," the gorgon said.

"Oh, no." Petra kept her grin in check, tempting as it was to flash her teeth. "You don't get to bend me over like Socrates at a symposium and then turn coy."

Emerald eyes narrowed. "Or you'll do what?"

"I'll do what I came here to do." She leaned in until her lips were a hairs-breadth from Medusa's, voice soft but gaze unblinking. "I'll steal."

"You were going to steal from me anyway," Medusa muttered, then placed a palm against Petra's breast and pushed. "Look to your heart's content. I doubt you will find anything that inter-ests you. Nothing a god designed, cer-tainly."

That final denial only heightened Pe-tra's curiosity. She turned over, rejoic-ing in the renewed counterweight of her tail, and crawled to the foot of the bed. The lid of the chest was still open, requiring her to lean over it and reach down, but that was no trouble compared to the other balancing acts the mountain had required.

Especially when the reward was a bird's eye view of Medusa's creativity, presented as a cornucopia of craft across disciplines and mediums. Leatherwork predominated, but there were signs of smithing, too, in burnished rings and restraints, as well as a stunning bronze weave intended to drape from throat to breast, feigning modesty from one angle and denying it from the rest. The gorgon's experiments in clay were limited to beads, some sealed with dyed cord threaded between them, slowly growing in size, and others fired and unfinished, as if she had not yet decided what to do with the lot.

But those were the top layers, hiding what lay underneath. Petra carefully displaced what she found, stacking Medusa's work to the left until reaching what appeared to be the bottom of the chest, lined with the hide of some other poor serpent. Yet she had seen the chest from the front and knew it went deeper, prompting Petra to run a nail along the inside edge until finding a gap that could be widened and pried upward.

Stones. Dozens upon dozens of stones. At least, that was what they initially appeared to be: primarily jaspers and jades, ranging from cool and polished black to ephemeral and almost translucent green, a select few banded with swirls of vermillion and ochre or dappled with pinpricks of white, like stars barely visible through the setting sun. While they ranged in weight, each one was utterly smooth, without rasps or cracks, not even the subtle seams of a geode to be found. It was the sort of perfection only found when rock tumbled through salt water for days on end, but the oblong shape was perfect, too, revealing an extra hand outside of nature.

They were eggs. Not real ones—Petra could feel from heft alone that the stone was solid the whole way through, with no separation between interior and shell—but carved to appear identically as such. Volcanic rock was in no short supply here, but the chosen materials came with their own tell: no poison or color could leach from this would-be clutch, whether they were exposed to water, heat, or something else.

She took one between her fingertips, its surface covered with overlapping orange and sepia rings like a leopard's spots, and brought the egg up into view before turning back toward Medusa. The gorgon had retreated to the headboard, her mouth set in a neutral line, but there was no hiding the wariness set in her posture, radiating through that lethal gaze. Petra's immunity did not lessen the burden of the other woman's stare, warning that there was only one right thing to say, and a thousand potential missteps surrounding the question.

"Were these for yourself or someone else?" she asked.

Medusa swallowed, then cleared her throat. "Myself."

"You've done stunning work." The sheer number of stones suggested *ob-*

session, although Petra did not say that aloud. "But why? What purpose do they serve?"

Silence severed the bed in two. Petra remained still, refusing to assume or raise a rhetorical shield in defense. In the cradle of her palm, the egg drank warmth from her skin, soaking through every side.

"I'm alone," Medusa finally said, still coiled, her entire body waiting to flinch. "*Medusa* is singular, barren. What Athena wrought upon me made my womb... incompatible with others. Perhaps it saved me in some way from Poseidon, but I was never given that choice, be it with another woman or through some sorcery."

Petra ran her thumb from the oblong tip of the egg down its flawless belly. "So you sculpted your dreams."

"Dreams. Fantasies." A lilt in the gorgon's tone elided the two, as if both would be equally possible in the right moment. "Something to grip tight when I could not hold onto anyone else."

For years, Petra held nothing but disdain at the thought of siring a child. What point was there when she represented a terminal bloodline, doomed to end whenever she finally succumbed to the inconvenience of death? When her body acted on instincts of old, responding to vestigial chemistry, the results of their alchemy were an incomparable torture. Agnodice's knife had been a balm, beyond what could be measured. But going to Cybele's temple had been a choice, not a second violation salting the wounds of the first like Medusa's.

And Petra's own discomfort with such activity was of the expected method, more than anything else. She turned the stone over between one finger and the next, picturing those wild lithic colors disappearing between the slick red petals of Medusa's cunt. The gorgon would be flush with exertion and arousal, the drum of her belly drawn full and taut. How might it sound when the other woman orgasmed over and over again in a new fertility rite, made for just the two of them?

Petra held the egg aloft for Medusa's inspection. "How many can you take?"

The caution in emerald eyes shattered against a surge of lust. "What?"

"How many?" she repeated. "At the same time."

"Six or seven, depending on the size." Medusa blushed, coaxing a shade of myrtle to her cheeks. "But I managed ten, once."

It was only through lifelong stoicism that Petra managed to keep from raising an eyebrow at that; better to hide how impressed she was than appear judgmental. "Sit back, grab the headboard, and spread your legs."

Half her command was obeyed—Medusa let the tension in her thighs go slack, and she leaned against the mother-of-pearl mosaic—before the gorgon paused to ask, "What are we doing?"

I'm giving you what you want would have been the simple answer, had Medusa phrased it as a simple question. But a greater, existential stress spun through the words, countless overlapping cords pulling at one another, grappling for meaning, trust, and a truly dangerous notion: permanence. To-gether they made a plea for more, using a vocabulary Petra had struggled with her entire life. She couldn't promise, but she could pretend.

The basilisk's lips parted in a smile, ravenous and knowing. "I don't know about you, but I'm wondering if there's a way to make you take eleven."

Medusa's full-body shiver was its own answer, as was the slow change in her posture, knees untangling and wrists resting against the cold carving of the ouroboros. "And why would you do that?"

"Why are you questioning me when you know what I came here for?" Petra rose up to her knees, putting the gorgon in her shadow. Emotion had bled from her voice, and what remained was ice, wreathed around imperious command.

"A queen has one purpose in the royal bed, does she not?"

The gorgon's breath caught, high and eager, before she composed her face into a mask of reluctance. "But we tried before..."

"We will try again," Petra snapped, injecting the cold with a core of bitterness. "We will try until my blood quickens inside of yours and you carry the clutch I wed you for. Is that understood?"

"Yes," Medusa said, scarcely above a whisper.

"Good." As she turned toward the chest again, Petra added, "then do as you were told."

After leaning over the lid to begin her search, Petra's tail swished with open impatience, the tip purposefully batting against one of the gorgon's feet.

Medusa recoiled, letting out a soft hiss, but the movement that followed was slow and deliberate, repositioning her body closer to the headboard.

The basilisk acted as if nothing had happened, taking in the trove under her hands to make a selection. Among the jaspers were several which must have been cut from the same larger piece, each resulting egg sharing a pattern like broken red glass, black and creamy white filaments of breccia interlaced with the gaps. She gathered the whole set—five in total—and placed them on the foot of the bed before deciding which others would be suitable.

A plum-colored jade was too beautiful to ignore, although it was one of the largest in Medusa's collection. Petra marked that for later use and chose two pale blue stones of a smaller size;

their color reminded her of snow on the peaks of Falakro Oros. The last three were a comfortable weight, sharing streaks of tumultuous greens and sunburst yellow, merging together only to stretch and twist into thin, fleeting tributaries.

Together on the bed, her chosen clutch looked like a pirate's ransom, untold wealth seized from every corner of the world. The basilisk spread them out between her fingers, letting smooth stone kiss stone, and turned toward Medusa to grab the open lekythos of oil. Petra nearly forgot her purpose at the sight of the other woman pressed against the headboard, hands poised at the top as if both wrists were shackled, lissome thighs spread and folded outward to meet the sheets. Caught between kneeling and hanging, waiting to surrender.

Their eyes met as Petra wet her fingertips, a few mere drops on each, and moved further up the bed using her knees. She drew a golden line from Medusa's lip to her chin, then anointed each breast in slow circles before spreading a light trail of oil along the gorgon's stomach and lower still.

"I leave no trust in Demeter or Persephone, so we must host our own thesmophoria, here and now," Petra said, never breaking Medusa's gaze, even when painting her clit with measured strokes. "I am both butcher and king, come to claim you as my own. We ascend together, fast together, and make sacrifice."

Medusa sucked in a breath when Petra's hand withdrew. "Can this body be purified?"

"It already is," Petra declared, reaching for the first egg, small and blue, easy to endure. "We are serpents, holy. Just because the world has forgotten to give us our due does not change what we stand for."

She dipped the egg in the neck of the lekythos, less measured this time, oiling the stone and her fingers to the knuckle. Medusa blinked and bit her lip as Petra closed the distance between their bodies, positioned within the cradle of strained thighs and above the gorgon's flexed torso.

"Bring your knees up," the basilisk ordered. When Medusa's obeisance was half-hearted, she added with a growl, "higher."

The shift forced Medusa's folds to part, exposing her cunt and the large, glistening swell of her clit. Petra teased the narrow tip of the egg against the gorgon's waiting entrance, watching conflicted pleasure flash through emerald eyes before she pushed it the rest of the way in. A pair of the basilisk's fingers followed, encouraging a wider stretch, and Medusa spat a curse, chased by a moan from the depths of her throat. Another thrust urged the egg past the limit of Petra's fingertips, deep as it could go, and her withdrawal was sedate, lasting as long as she could before slipping out again.

"There's no need to struggle yet." Petra reached back for the second egg, twin to the first, and doused it just the same, lubrication dripping past the line of her knuckles. "This is only the beginning."

Defiance, raucous and bright, put a harsh gleam on Medusa's eyes. Her jaw clenched as Petra eased that stone inside, too, adding a third finger to the adjoining thrust. Salt and musk clung to the air, intensified by the fluids clinging to the basilisk's digits, the sound of coupling slowed to a ritual tenor.

Empty-handed once more, Petra glanced away to take stock of her clutch. This time she chose a larger egg with its brilliant jasper shell, and held it up to Medusa like a captive on display. "Ten like this, or like the others? I wonder if you're cruel or kind to yourself alone."

The other woman didn't answer, but her eyes pursued the egg when Petra rubbed its cooler surface against her cunt, the contact shaking a gasp from the gorgon's lips. Petra teased further, rolling the smaller end around Medusa's clit, red tempting red. Only when Medusa's hips jerked did Petra relent, tilting the egg downward so it could start to slip inside. At halfway, Medusa clenched, resistance stalling Petra's fingers, the widest part of the stone trapped just outside of where it was meant to be.

"Don't make me force you," the basilisk warned.

Medusa bared her fangs. "I make you do nothing."

Five mere words wove a complex tapestry, a warp of shame and weft of pride, waiting to be torn down in unison. Petra's palm curved around the bottom of the egg, leverage guiding it past that point of tension, pushing inside Medusa even as she clawed at the headboard and shouted in protest. The sound was snuffed out by a sudden exhale when Petra tested her with four fingers this time, exacting pressure from knuckle to knuckle.

"You can't—" she began breathlessly.

"I can do as I please, queen of mine," Petra uttered, reading the topography of a dozen stifled expressions. "Or do you forsake me?"

The gorgon cycled through several long breaths, and with the last of them, relaxed around Petra's hand to allow her access. Yet only when she pushed deep and parted her digits, demanding more, did Medusa's answer come, lighter than a whisper amidst a storm.

"Never."

Three eggs were enough to meet at the farthest point within her, a growing and undeniable weight. But plenty of space remained around Petra's fingers, so she reached for two more of the jaspers, her entire palm now slick. She fed the first of the trio into Medusa's cunt slow and deep, then leaned down to suck at the gorgon's clit in pace with the second stone.

Medusa moaned, thrashing against the headboard, and reflexively squeezed around the glistening batch inside her to no avail. They held her open to Petra's ministrations, the fork of the basilisk's tongue working in quick strokes, four fingers moving in rough tandem, demanding more with every pass. When Petra finally withdrew her hand again, Medusa made a primal, frustrated noise, caught between denial and ecstasy.

"Quiet," Petra hissed, even as she sought another, larger egg, capturing the jade carving in the loop of her tail to bring it farther up the bed and into reach. "That's only five. Unless you were lying to me. And you wouldn't do that, gorgon—would you?"

"I did not lie," Medusa choked out.

Yet a sound closer to a whimper fled her throat as Petra began to slide the sixth egg inside, Medusa's thighs visibly trembling with each swollen centimeter. Her breath quickened, eyes fluttering closed, and Petra returned to lavish worship, trading swift circles around the other woman's labia and clit for languid suction, deep pulls matching a deeper thrust. When the jade escaped her grasp, settling in with the rest, that sudden friction made release inevitable.

It was a shaking, furious sort of orgasm, Medusa's feet digging into the bed like talons, tendons flaring across her arms and shoulders, standing out in relief along her elegant neck. Every cry of pleasure ended on a jagged *ah*, plucked from her lungs and increasing in pitch. Petra savored the sound, casting aside the colors and shapes of her vision to focus on the bloom of heat spreading from Medusa's belly, nacreous rings spinning out over one another in a continuous prismatic loop.

The basilisk's mouth broke contact, clear arousal streaked down the pale stretch of her chin. "That was six. Now for the rest."

"No!" Medusa snarled, although her hands remained slack atop the headboard. "No, you can't, I already—"

Petra silenced her with a glare. Anyone else would have dropped dead, but the gorgon's pupils only dilated further, eclipsed by desire. "We are not done."

When she took another jade in hand, this one was so translucent green it looked softer than its fellows, a kind of clarity found in jellyfish and other floating creatures of the sea. Yet there was no mistaking the egg's size as Petra urged it between oversensitive folds, the first lingering contact drawing a strangled sort of noise from Medusa. Much to her surprise, the gorgon's struggle quieted after that, body full and flush with afterglow, accepting the intrusion in the wake of untold bliss. The eighth sank inside with ease, too, even though its presence created a greater curve along Medusa's stomach.

The ninth was where she began to fight again, leveling Petra with a glowering stare, half challenge and half disbelief. Her body echoed the rebellion, drawing tight enough for an ache to radiate back through the basilisk's fingers. But rather than retreat, Petra began to press the tip of the egg against a ridged spot high within the other woman's cunt, building intensity with faint twists of her wrist. Medusa hissed, back arching as a rush of liquid warmth met Petra's hand, enough wetness to tuck her thumb against her palm and have that fit inside too.

It did not matter how many times she had done this. There was no escaping the simple miracle of watching her fist—so often a tool of destruction, the place where violence left her body and entered the world—disappear inside someone, nor the elation and shock that always followed this sort of joining. Not out of pain but sheer vigor, entered and explored in such an incomparable way. Even the most skilled cock couldn't reach for five places at once; that part of the body lacked the curve and drive of the wrist, achieving unmatched depth with the grace of a limb used a thousand times over.

"Gods take you!" Medusa gripped the headboard with such force, Petra wasn't sure if her nails or the ouroboros carving would shatter first. "Petra, it's too much."

"Is it?" She waited another breath for the answer, and when no further refusal came, her hand sank deeper, one blood-tinged scale at a time. "Now that can't be true. Feel how you're taking me in, how full you can be? We need a dynasty to rule the world again, and that starts with you. Right here. With a basilisk's brood."

The gorgon spat a curse that Petra hadn't heard for the better part of a thousand years, but Medusa's entire body pulsed around her fist, clenching and trying to lure her further. Only when the basilisk's knuckles brushed over the gathered eggs did she start to pull back, just as careful, just as disciplined. When her wrist met open air again, Petra paused, watching Medusa squeeze against the breadth of her hand before reaching back with the other to fetch the tenth egg, fractured green and blooming gold.

She wedged it into the slick curve of her palm, using the cage of her fingers to ease the taper of the stone into Medusa's waiting cunt. The stretch deepened as the egg passed from one hand to another, and the gorgon trembled from head to toe, the serpents atop her head echoing their mistress' building tension, hissing and wild. When Petra slowly folded her hand into a fist again, bringing her knuckles against that same spot from a moment before, there was no need to push the egg deeper—Medusa surrendered with a shout.

This orgasm rippled under her skin, overwrought muscles jumping and twitching, ecstasy hollowing out her throat. Petra applied no pressure save for the length of her other arm across Medusa's hips; the sublime weight she carried held her in place like a lodestone. The gorgon's release was longer than her first, but every throb came closer together, wet heat drenching Petra nearly to the elbow.

She waited until the worst of the thrashing settled before drawing soothing circles over the low strain of Medusa's belly and pressing a kiss to the corner of her hip. "One more."

"You're mad," the gorgon managed between staccato breaths. "We both are."

"And isn't that why our blood is destined to meet?" Petra whispered, the tip of her tail wrapping around the final egg so it could be nudged close enough for her to take. "Give this to me and be free."

There were no words after that. The lightest tap of the egg against Medusa's clit sent her spiraling into another release, and Petra ceased to count—three, five, perhaps more—as she offered the very last of the clutch, for the pulses around her fist were constant now, indistinguishable from each other as Medusa's moans broke down into terse, visceral sounds, wholly feral compared to her previous screams. A chant of unmaking and rebirth, flayed by ecstasy only to be stitched into the earth again.

Emerald eyes rolled back, the gorgon's chest snapping upward like she had been struck by a swarm of arrows from behind, pierced through. Her grip along the headboard failed as she collapsed against the bed, unable to endure, no longer driven to pretend. When the rising fervor of her voice died down, Petra felt deafened, for the inhales and exhales afterward were so quiet, it was as if Medusa's very lungs had wilted.

"They should come out now," Petra said. "Can I do that?"

The other woman managed a nod, holding onto consciousness by a thread.

With euphoria slackening her face and glazed across her eyes, Petra didn't push for Medusa to answer aloud; rest was a better remedy in the aftermath.

Her work was slow—every so often, certain nerves were so sensitive she had to wait for Medusa to settle again—but Petra retrieved the eggs in companionable silence, quietly awestruck that the gorgon had taken so much. After the last of the clutch slipped free, Petra's hand followed suit one finger at a time, but even that measured pace didn't stop Medusa from hissing in dismay when she was finally empty.

No, not a hiss. A sob.

The basilisk's eyes flickered upward, wary of seeing something she shouldn't, but no rage or rejection rose as her eyes met Medusa's again. Tears flowed down the gorgon's face, twin rivers becoming a subtle water-fall as they dripped past her jaw. Petra's tongue stilled, unsure of what she could say to offer comfort—if she even had the right—but when she opened her arms in a silent offering, the other woman lunged, almost crushing herself against Petra's breast.

Some part of her waited for the press of fangs or sting of venom. Instead, Medusa hid against the gentle curve of Petra's throat, both arms wrapped around the column of her back, un-yielding. Black and white scales alike, wet with tears and wet with sex, shone bright as Petra returned the powerful embrace, nuzzling the nest of serpents beneath her chin to soothe them too. And if she wept as well, for a moment, what of it? It wasn't poison, not any-more.

When the rivers dried to trails of salt, Petra asked, "Are you hurt?"

"No." Medusa's answer was soft but immediate. "People wound me for sport. That is much easier to bear than what we just did. Did I hurt you?"

A faint smile rose to the basilisk's lips. "Only in the ways I asked for. And I believe my question was answered in full."

"Mine wasn't." Lacquered nails drew an absent sigil around Petra's heart. "Who are you to arrive in such a way? How can you be the only one left?"

Centuries of mistakes. A millennia of misfortune. Gods and mortals were both to blame, but neither were the only true reason. The world no longer had a place for one such as her, not when she was an enemy to the ever-growing cage they called civilization. As to why she had survived when the rest of her generation had not—

"Because I hid. I learned to blend in, learned what was expected. Stature, language, what I wore and the way I wore it."

Medusa hummed softly in acknowledgement. "You named yourself, did you not?"

So she had noticed. Petra had built this moment into a terror, fed the revelation years and years of fear, only for the gorgon to ask like it was any other question. "Of course. Even your tongue could not say my true name. That language died with my mother and her last clutch."

Petra often wished she could have grown up under her mother's aegis, but birthing that final den killed her in the effort, corpse holding heat just long enough for the new eggs to hatch. Two of Petra's would-be siblings had languished in the shell anyway, but a fatal beginning was a mercy compared to the excruciating decades it took the rest of them to die, be it by slaughtering each other in misplaced jealousy, or goading heroes into blood feuds. Her oldest brother, facing eternity, had taken his own life once the others were gone, seeing their loss as proof of his own failed fatherhood.

But she refused to surrender to that annihilating urge. No matter how she suffered in silence, Petra knew there had to be some reason the spark of her soul persisted. That ever-fervent flame was waiting for something.

Perhaps for this very moment.

She was *comfortable*. Even with blood drying on the sheets and a goddess' demand hanging over her head, countless years of agony ripped from her soul and thrown out into the open, Petra could never remember finding this singular calm anywhere else—with anyone else.

And the basilisk longed for more. How could a single taste satisfy after an eon of denial? To share another woman's private bed, to exist in her home as if she was always meant to be there, was like a new star suddenly splitting the sky, offering direction in the dark where none had ever been before. The light stung, almost terrifying in its intensity, but closing her eyes against that glow risked extinguishing it forever.

How long had she hid? How much time had she already wasted looking away?

"Were there others?" Petra asked, wrestling herself back into the present. She should have said *what do you want now* but the question itself was a brand, too hot to touch. "Before Athena. Before the Lord of the Sea came for you."

"Many," the gorgon admitted, absent shame. "When my father Phorcys died in battle, I was left to rule in his place. My beauty attracted countless suitors, although I had no intent to wed. I wanted women and my island and freedom. But my throne lay between Poseidon's ocean and a stream sacred to Athena's virginal gaze."

Bitterness coated Petra's tongue. "You were punished."

"Maybe. Or maybe I was just a lark on that summer day, spied naked and half-asleep. It's impossible to know with gods if you mean everything or nothing at all."

A brazen yet unsettling point. Petra had not put much thought as to why Cybele chose her over some other supplicant, because she was so used to being bargained for and sent elsewhere. She liked to think the Great Mother showed more generosity in her affections, but was there any way to be sure?

"You can take them," Medusa said softly.

The basilisk blinked. "What?"

"Perseus' spoils. His lot is yours to surrender to Cybele." Medusa leaned back just far enough for Petra to see warm green eyes again. "The last thing I want is you also being cursed by a goddess for breaking a pact."

Petra had forgotten about the artifacts entirely. "You're sure?"

"I keep his head." A wry smile pushed past the other woman's obvious exhaustion. "It's no use to anyone without the rest of him anyway. But deliver the gods' gifts as you please. I won't stop you."

A fair deal, Petra thought. She couldn't imagine plucking the disparate bits of Perseus out of the walls to begin with, but Hades had the man's spirit already, so the flesh couldn't be of greater concern. Even if tears came more easily now, she would not waste them on the fool who had come to slaughter Medusa. The divine would return to the divine, and no more.

"Thank you," she said.

Despite her own fatigue, Petra sat up and stretched, extending her arms as far as they would go, head proud and legs braced. She was about to climb out of bed when Medusa stopped her with a sudden grip around the wrist.

"I was not sending you away by saying that." The gorgon's tone was, of all things, riddled with anxiety. "You should at least stay long enough to sleep. We are so very alike, after all."

Petra had given in when Idalia made the same entreaty to rest, but the priestess never intended to keep her. A passing in the night carried similarly fleeting risk; her joining with Antheia, and the temple girls, and so many other women lost to time, dragged danger close, only to flee from any waiting consequence the moment their shared ardor cooled. She knew of no other way to survive.

Except the look in the gorgon's eyes asked for more. The delicate thread now woven between them was sure to

find another anchor, and another, forming a braid even tighter than the Phry-
gians' fabled knot. They could protect
each other; they could make something
that would outlive betrothals and king-
doms.

What a temptation. Greater than
temptation, Petra realized, a desire
which wore a crown called *compulsion*
and threatened indomitable rule. This
bed was fit for two, and there were no
responsibilities on the whole of Sarpedon save what affection might ask for.
On an island unmoored from time, only
spoken of in legend or rumor, who
would come looking for them now that
Perseus was dead?

Cybele, first and foremost. While Petra would accept the goddess' wrath
upon herself, letting it afflict Medusa
too was cruelty compounded. Better to

shield the other woman the best way she could than damn them both to further retribution.

But how to say such a thing without gutting herself all over again?

"If I sleep, I may do more than stay," Petra said softly. "And I will not demand such an obligation from the woman I came to rob."

"I forgive you," Medusa answered in her next breath, "but I won't chain you to this rock like Prometheus, either."

Petra got to her feet before she could think better of it. She gathered the kibisis first, glancing inside briefly to confirm both of Hermes' sandals were there before slinging the strap over her shoulder. When she knelt to do the same with her xiphos and scabbard, the basilisk suddenly remembered what was missing.

"Where is his sword?" she asked.

"Ah, yes." Medusa rose halfway to her knees and reached over the back of the headboard. Metal clicked before she drew out the blade, a short length of adamantine in the harpe style, ending with a shallow sickle's curve at the very tip. Every edge was brutally sharp, and possessed a dire crystalline hue. "I hung it here, for protection."

It had been within her reach the entire time. Petra wasn't sure whether to be amused, relieved, or grateful as she took the weapon from the gorgon's hand. "With all I have to carry, it's a good thing you gave me back my tail. Do you care if I take the shield from its frame?"

"No. Your way out is behind the mirror anyway."

Petra was wholly stunned for the better part of a breath. "There's another way out? I thought I was going to have to carry this entire burden over lava and more."

The gorgon laughed—that gorgeous laugh, better than any Muse plying their trade—and shook her head. "Do you think I crawl through a gauntlet of fangs and bones every morning to greet the day? The other path is smaller and hidden away, of course, but torture is for strangers, not guests."

Still somewhat dazed by the revelation, Petra walked to the shield-turned-mirror and lifted it from the bronze frame. Behind the reflective metal were lines cut into the stone wall, same as the rising door she had passed to reach this chamber. Another dark plate had been incised along the floor, waiting for a body's pressure to open it.

"Don't forget the helmet," Medusa added softly. "Unless you need me to find it for you."

She should have said yes, given the other woman a reason to rise and press close to her again, but this was already difficult, and Petra could not bear adding another weight to the balance. "No need. That demigod's stench is a dead giveaway."

Hades' helm appeared the moment she freed it from Perseus' frigid head. She marveled at how familiar the cap appeared between her hands before storing it in the kibisis too, feathers upon feathers. Not having to traverse halls full of traps a second time would preserve her in life and limb, but her armor had been abandoned there, and her shield and spear, objects which meant far more to the basilisk than anything a god could forge.

They would have to be one last sacrifice, the second skin of humanity she had worn for so long left as a warning for others, should any dare to set foot on this island and seek the woman down below. If someone happened to approach on her way back to the temple, Petra reasoned she could use the helm to make herself invisible long enough to escape attention. After that, she would—

Her throat tightened; better not to think of what lay so far ahead now.

"Fare well," is what Petra forced herself to say, "and perhaps forgive me once more for the state of your sheets."

"You promised me ruin in return," Medusa said. The gorgon's gaze had drifted into the distance, leveled on a mirror that was no longer there. "So there is nothing to forgive."

Though Petra was laden by Olympian bounty, no other difficulties or trials were to be found in the quiet tunnel through the mountain. The ease of it only intensified her regret. It was a dark and simple slope of obsidian, tilting ever upward until she emerged through a curtain of vines on the other side. Plant life flourished here in a way it hadn't where the tribute boat was bound, like a secret garden was being kept out of sight from all but the sea.

She needed said boat to return, so Petra began to march through the boscage of bushes and cypress, keeping the mountain to her left as she followed the curve of the island toward its blackened beach. The sun hung high and seductive, its unleashed heat soaking into her naked body the same way Medusa had. Part of her wanted to lay out across the sand until eventide came, drinking in paradise as if it could be stored like water in a camel's hump, providing sustenance in more hostile climes. Part of her wanted to turn around and run back down into the heart of the mountain, fast as her feet could carry her, and damn the gods if they got in her way.

But not a single component of Petra Kruos, from bone to soul, had expected the divine beast dozing next to the tribute boat when its hand-carved bow came into view.

The lioness possessed a hide so white and magnificent it spun the sun into countless colors wherever light met lustrous fur. Her body was fat and strong, first to hunt and first to eat, and of such marvelous size that she was longer than the ship itself when measured from paws to tail. The only interruption of the lioness' lovely physique was the single band of a golden harness, with a loop forged along the top so it could be joined to a yoke with ease.

Petra froze, but her stillness did not prevent the lioness from rousing. Dark and holy eyes, the black of meteoric iron, opened and pierced her through. She expected a fight, but waited to draw her sword; Perseus' might have been a better-suited blade, yet the idea of using his weapon in a moment of terror put an acrid taste in the basilisk's mouth.

The lioness rose and stretched, but did not take a step forward. She did not even have to speak, for recognition thrilled Petra to the core. This was one of the very creatures who pulled Cybele's chariot, a living symbol of her power over the wilderness, nature untrammeled by the dominion of mortal kind.

"Mother of the mountains," Petra said, fitting her words with care and respect. "Mistress of animals. As your servant granted the change I sought, I have brought the favor you asked for."

She set Athena's shield down first, then slipped the strap of the kibisis off her shoulder. The sword was laid in place last, its adamant blade capturing the sun like the lioness' pelt, swallowing glory before reflecting it back upon the air. Petra took a step back, her hands open and empty.

One massive paw moved, then the next. The lioness walked at a ponderous pace, as if waiting for Petra to either lash out or run. Yet she did neither, even as huge yellow fangs were revealed and the lioness took the top of the shield between her jaws, pulling it and the other artifacts into sacred custody.

Except the beast also stood between Petra and the ship, and when the basilisk took a step toward where the tribute was stacked, those iron eyes narrowed in ancient challenge. No further translation was needed.

Where are you going?

Away, Petra almost said. Elsewhere. Some land past the fishing village and the temple and every named city she had ever known. Surely there was a place where the worst of humankind had yet to press their stamp upon the earth, that she could live in unmarked solitude for a while longer. Culling away her true form again was no longer an option; she didn't want to hide, she wanted to be *known*, but that was the most dangerous endeavor of them all. Perhaps she could found a coterie for other women like herself, ever-threatened, and protect them in a way her own mother never had the chance to do. They could blossom and laugh and fall in love without fearing a world that refused to understand such beauty.

The lioness' baleful gaze left Petra, drawing a line between the tribute boat and the mountain.

"Here," the basilisk said under her breath, wary of putting volume to the words and solidifying the idea in her mind. "I could have that here. With her."

Leonine nature lacked the capacity to smile, but the prideful glow in tenebrous eyes felt much the same. What was lost could be restored, had Petra the courage to confront what she feared the most—opening her heart to that waiting hand again. Medusa could certainly say no.

But had she not already said yes, the moment she asked Petra to stay and sleep?

"I still need the tribute," Petra said to the lioness. "Those are gifts sworn to her. But the ship will stay right where it is."

After a long and teasing yawn, the beast stepped aside. Petra did not hesitate, stepping off the beach and into the ocean so she could gather the boxes stacked in the back of the boat. Water lapped persistently at the basilisk's calves as she discerned how to carry the entire trove at once, using her tail to brace what could not be leveled against her back or upon each shoulder. The final phial of oil hung from its merchant's cord between Petra's teeth.

She broke troth with the horizon and faced the mountain. She walked, lighter than air, to where the second spark of her soul lay awake, waiting against all hope for the basilisk's return.

Acknowledgements

I'm grateful to Landice, Ladz, Morgan, Devi, and Rien (the other one!) for their in-depth feedback, beta comments, blurbs, and encouragement for this book. What started out as the simple concept of 'snake lesbians?' grew into something far more complex, and Petra and Medusa's story would not be the same without you.

Also by Rien Gray

THE OUT OF TRUE SERIES

Valerin the Fair

Martis the Brazen

Seure the Tempered

THE FATAL FIDELITY SERIES

Love Kills Twice

Love Bleeds Deep

Love Burns Bright

A Love So Dark

STANDALONES
A Strip of Velvet

Double Exposure

Her Wolf in the Wild

Summaries, purchase links, and content notes are available at riengray.com.

www.ingramcontent.com/pod-product-compliance
Lightning Source LLC
Chambersburg PA
CBHW051951150726
47999CB00004B/1333